Unbranded

Montana Bred Series
Book 1

LINDA BRADLEY

Akin House Publishing

DEDICATION

For all the girls and women who prefer cowboy boots over high heels.

ACKNOWLEDGMENTS

Thank you to my *Montana Bound Series* readers who fell in love with the band of misfit characters as much as I did. Who knew that when Chloe and John McIntyre moved in next door to Maggie Abernathy, their story would see Chloe grow into a determined young woman ready to run her grandfather's Montana ranch?

Thank you to the wonderful Julie Sturgeon for editing **Unbranded**. Your suggestions and expertise brought new dimension to Chloe and the world she lives in.

Thank you to my writing pals—the Babes. You've made this writing journey one to remember. You whole-heartedly excel at brainstorming— and so many other things that inspire me.

Thank you to Nan Rowe for making my vision a reality. Your impeccable design and eye for color captures Chloe and her world to a tea. The cover is gorgeous!

Thank you to the MMRWA members and Greater Detroit Romance Writers for your support and friendship.

Thank you to my family for letting me be me. Near or far, you're always in my heart!

Praise for the Montana Bound Series

Maggie's Way (Montana Bound Series Book 1)

"Linda Bradley's fresh voice will keep readers riveted from beginning to end. Bradley delivers a heart-warming story full of disarming honesty and beautiful drama…This one stands out!"

—*Jane Porter, New York Times and USA Today Best Seller, author of Flirting with Forty and It's You*

"Maggie's Way is a heart-warming tale of love and loss, fear and friendship. With charming characters and a moving plot, Linda Bradley's lovely debut gently reminds us that it's never too late for second chances."

—*Lori Nelson Spielman, international best seller, author of The Love List and Sweet Forgiveness*

The Romance Reviews Readers' Choice Awards Finalist

Greater Detroit Booksellers' Best Award Finalist

A Montana Bound Christmas: Ho, Ho, Home for the Holidays!
(Montana Bound Series Book 4)

"What fun! From the first chapter to the last, this story is a like a warm hug. Linda Bradley weaves the different worlds of each of the characters together in a rich tapestry that mirrors the story line itself. This could easily become a beloved holiday movie classic."
—*Annette Rochelle Aben, #1 best seller*

"If you like your holiday romance with a lot of feel-good emotions, you'll really enjoy this continuation of the Montana Bound series."
—*Nancy Fraser, award-winning Author*

"Ms. Bradley has produced another delightful read…a Christmas gift for all of us."
—*Joanne Guidoccio, author of Too Many Women in the Room*

"If you've read the Montana Bound series, this is a welcome addition, and if you haven't – you can read it as a standalone, but to get the full impact of what these characters have been through, start at the beginning, *Maggie's Way*."
—*Cyrene Olson, Uncaged Book Reviews*

CHAPTER 1

I PEED ON the stick and said a prayer.

I wasn't sure which stirred the queasy flutter in my belly, the fact I could be pregnant or the fact I'd have to own the responsibility. Matt and I weren't ready for an addition. We'd been friends since college. We never talked about marriage, and I liked it that way.

My toe-tapping didn't speed up the process. I wiped my sweaty palms on my jeans. The stopwatch on my phone ticked like the stride of a sloth. I wrapped the pregnancy test in tissue, tucked it beneath the washcloths in the vanity drawer, peeked into the hallway, then decided to go downstairs to the kitchen. I stuck my head in the refrigerator. The blast of air cooled my brow. My stomach rolled over.

My relationship with Matt wouldn't ever be the same.

I grabbed a bottle of water, shut the door, and twisted the top off. The plastic container crackled. With an eye on the clock, I drummed my fingertips on the counter. The granite was cold, unforgiving.

I peered out the picture window. Maggie and Dad were nowhere in sight. The midday sun lit the majestic Montana landscape. Dad had brought me here to live on his parents' 617 Ranch when I was eight—6/17, my grandparents' wedding date.

"I miss you, Grandpa," I whispered to his spirit and pictured him, the way he looked when I came here eighteen years ago. I wiped away brimming tears, turned on a heel, hurried back to the bathroom, and locked the world out.

I never knew my grandma, Ida May, and I wished I had. I'd seen her in old photographs and always wondered what part of me was like her. If any. And did she watch over me with my granddad?

My hands shook as I read the results on the white plastic stick. My vision blurred. There was no mistake about the outcome. I leaned against the counter and glanced in the mirror. I didn't feel twenty-six and pregnant.

The knock at the door jarred me. I took a deep breath, wrapped the evidence in toilet paper, then buried it beneath the existing trash.

"Chloe, are you in there?"

I turned on the water, washed my hands, and took a seat on the toilet to search the far crevices of my mind for an answer. Every problem had a solution. All I had to do was find it. Maggie called my name, again. My heart raced.

"Just a second." I pounded my fists into my thighs. The hangnail on my pointer finger caught in the fray of my blue jeans, and I bit my lip.

"Chloe? I could use your help." She paused. "Chloe," Maggie's voice was muffled through the heavy door. "Are you okay?"

"Yes." I dried my damp cheeks, stood, shook out my legs, and inspected myself in the mirror. My wavy, dishwater blond hair framed my flushed cheeks. The silver necklace I wore flickered in the light.

"I'm coming." I steadied my hand and reached for the doorknob.

Maggie stood in the hallway, leaning against the railing. Her lips pinched when our gazes met. I hoped I could hide my secret behind a smile. "What's going on?"

She stepped closer, the corners of her eyes her lined with concern. She was beautiful as ever, perhaps even more beautiful than when I first met her. Her slender fingers pushed strands of hair from my face.

Maggie tucked her long, strawberry blond hair behind her ears. I didn't think she'd ever go gray. I desperately wanted to ask her how it felt to carry a child.

"What's wrong, Chloe?"

My shoulders fell forward. What was I going to do with a baby? Maggie stroked my hair.

"Chloe, what's wrong?"

I had no words. Maggie held my hands in hers. The flecks of gold in her green irises shimmered like an Irish field as the light streamed through the window at the end of the hallway.

"It's nothing."

"You're obviously upset. You're shaking."

"Matt and I had an argument." I lowered my gaze at this lie.

"About what?"

Maggie examined me through narrow slits. Hopefully, she wouldn't go all Maggie on me. That's what Dad called it when she sensed something was off. As amusing as I thought it was when she turned the tides on him, I didn't want to be in the undertow should she suspect a fissure in my world. She had the nose of a hound when it came to pretense. I suspected she acquired this inherent sense before retiring from her elementary teaching career.

"I should talk to Matt first," I answered.

I swallowed away the knot at the back of my

throat and leaned against the wall. My shoulders fell forward. I tucked my fingers in my pockets and hooked my thumbs through the belt loops of my faded jeans.

My flat stomach wouldn't be so flat much longer.

"I can't imagine anything being so bad. You and Matt get along so well."

I leaned back; my shoulder blades skimmed the wall. "Yeah, I'm sure we can work it out." How do you work out a baby?

"I could use your help in the barn. Butch and Sundance have gotten into the burrs. I tried combing their tails, but they aren't having it. Thought maybe you could win them over with your charm and sugar."

I scuffed my boot lightly against the floor. "Butch and Sundance always find the burrs." So did I.

"Yes, they do"—Maggie smiled—"but they make up for their *horseplay* with hard work and loyalty."

"Nice one," I said, following her downstairs and into the main part of the house filled with rustic furnishings, love, and everything Montana. Pretty soon it would be filled with the pitter-patter of little feet.

"I'm sure whatever it is, it isn't as bad as you think. It's easy to make a mountain out of a molehill." Maggie stopped at the bottom of the stairs and turned to face me. "When you want to talk, I'm here."

"Thank you," I said.

"Do you feel like helping me?" She picked up Dad's corduroy barn jacket from the floor and hung it on the antler hall tree.

"Yeah, I can't let Butch and Sundance stay gnarled and knotted like your momma's knitting yarn."

"Speaking of my mom, I'd love to see her, up close and in person. I sure miss her." Maggie straightened the plaid throw on the back of the leather sofa. "Your dad's in the pasture rounding up cattle with the guys. Butch and Sundance have also been rolling in the mud. I can't wait 'til someone fills in the hole they've made. You'd swear they were a couple of wallowing hogs."

She stopped short in front of me, and I bumped into her. "Sorry," I said.

"No need to be sorry. I'm used to it. You've been on my heels since the day I met you. Remember the time we bumped heads and I needed stitches?"

"How could I forget?"

Maggie pushed the hair away from her left temple. "The scar is completely gone, but the memory lives on, dear girl."

There was a message in her words. She wasn't one to hold a grudge. She was making a point.

"I figured if I brought it up again, it would take your mind off whatever is troubling you. Michigan seems like a lifetime ago."

"Sure does," I said. "Some days I'd give anything to be a little girl again."

Maggie's gait across the dark planked floors was slow and easy. Over the years, she had absorbed our Gallatin Valley tempo of living and tamed her Midwestern suburban ways, but she hadn't forgotten her roots. When she wasn't riding or doing chores, she photographed ranching life in Montana with hopes of publishing her images in a coffee table book.

I turned off the kitchen lights and put on my cowboy hat. Maggie reached for me and squeezed my hands. Her soft touch melted my insides.

"I miss those days, too. I think I got the better end of the deal though," she said.

"Why's that?"

"Because I inherited you after the diapers, colic, and ear infections. I might've missed the baby and toddler years, but you were still young enough to cuddle with when I married your dad."

"Actually, *I think* I got the better end of the deal. You've made life easier. Having you made up for my mom's absence." I hugged her. "Mom's Hollywood modeling career has taken a toll on both of us. Me and her. Maybe someday she and I can make up for lost time, mend some of the rifts. She's always busy though." I opened the mudroom door. Samson, our scrappy bulldog, waited for us outside. He was seven but had the heart of a pup. "Come on, boy, let's get to the barn and see what's going on. If it weren't for me, this place would go under." Samson woofed and lollygagged down the path beside me. "I swear this dog is Bones reincarnated," I said to Maggie. "He has the same swagger and muddy brown eyes."

"Hey, what do you want for dinner tonight? I picked up some thick cowboy steaks at the butcher's today. How's that sound?"

She tripped on a rock and grabbed my arm to balance herself.

"Maybe." I shrugged.

"Geez, you must really be down in the dumps. Steak is your favorite."

"Steak sounds delicious. Wish Grandpa were here to cook. I wish he were here to do lots of things." What I wanted most was to curl up in his lap and bury my head in his shoulder. At the end of the day, whether I'd screwed up or not, I was *his* girl. And with him gone, I didn't quite fit in anymore. Somehow, Grandpa always made me feel like one of the guys. Dad, Grandpa, and I had been the three amigos. The banter came easily, and our intentions flowed freely in his presence. "I can't believe it's been almost two years," I said.

"Seems like yesterday, most days." Maggie blew a kiss toward his memorial marker up on the ridge, then whistled for Samson to get out of her garden. "His method of harvesting beets and carrots makes for a slim crop. He's got to stop digging holes."

Samson wasn't the only one digging holes. I looked toward the ridge where we'd scattered Grandpa's ashes. The shimmy down my spine forced my shoulders back, and I lifted my chin to the breeze. In my mind, my grandmother appeared to be nudging Grandpa out of the way. "You know what, Maggie? I'll cook."

"You sure? Your last attempt resulted in a near four-alarm fire."

"I'm positive—and thanks for the reminder. I put the last fire out, and I'll extinguish the ones to come." I tucked my fingers in my back pockets. A baby might fill Grandpa's void, but the sole way to make sure his legacy lived on was to take today's bull by the horns and wrestle it to the ground. I'd dreamed of running the ranch, not raising a child. I was being given a chance to follow in my grandmother Ida May's footsteps, which meant it was time to quit bellyaching about what I couldn't change and do something about the things I could. The McIntyre ranch had an heir on the way, and I was speaking for both of us now.

CHAPTER 2

DAD AND MAGGIE discussed hiring another ranch hand during dinner. I cut my steak into neat squares and ate the pieces one by one. I pushed the peas around on my plate like I was rounding up strays. If I didn't invite myself into the conversation, no one else would.

My grandmother wouldn't have stayed silent during business discussions.

"Excuse me." I squared my shoulders. "I think it's time I started making more decisions with you regarding the ranch."

Dad rubbed his whiskery chin. "I'm not sure the rest of us are ready for that."

"With all due respect, I beg to differ. I'm here for the long haul." I paused. "I could even be your co-CEO. I know the ranch inside and out. Delegating some of the work would free up your schedule." I sat a little taller. "We'd work well together. That's for sure. I'd be a great co-CEO."

"Chloe, I didn't help your granddad make decisions until we moved back here. I had a lot of schooling and a whole lot of life under my belt. Practicing medicine taught me more than how to care for people."

"Dad, I've been watching you and Grandpa do business since I was eight. I'd say that's a whole lot of schooling, too."

Dad glanced at Maggie then back to me.

"Let's take this one step at a time." He reached over and patted my hand. "We've got plenty of time to discuss you taking the reins. It's going to be awhile before I hang up my spurs. I'd like to hear your thoughts on hiring another wrangler though."

"We should. Grandpa's been gone for two years, and Trout's growing older. He really should lighten his load, but who knows if he'll ever admit it." I paused. "We could definitely use another solid, hired hand around here. Justin's taking fall classes at the university again. He'll commute when he can, but when the coursework really kicks in, he'll stay there. Matt and Quinn keep the animals in line, but we need more hands. We can't shy on maintenance if we want to maintain our standards. We need someone who can jump on board without batting an eyelash and who understands our philosophy of ranching. We're really moving cattle and horses. The more animals we move, the greater the revenue." I took in

Maggie's approving nod. The gurgle in my belly reminded me I wasn't just advocating for the better of the ranch.

"Great, we'll start looking," Dad replied. "That was quite the delivery."

"I'll help in any way I can," I said. I'd do more than help. I pushed the last few peas onto my fork with my knife.

"There's huckleberry ice cream in the freezer." Maggie ate the last bite of her steak. "Anyone else ready for dessert?"

I cleared the plates and took them into the kitchen. They clunked against the counter as I set them next to the sink. My stomach dipped and swayed. The waves of nausea were sporadic; hopefully, they'd end soon. Dad rested his hand on my shoulder. The warmth from his touch penetrated my cotton shirt. "Want some ice cream?" I asked.

"If there's something wrong, I'd like to know," he said. "You look pale." The corners of his mouth drew downward.

"Thanks, but I'm fine. Today's been weird. Lots to think about." *A weird week, a weird month, a weird everything.* "A new guy will be good." Contemplating the reality of juggling a child and being Dad's co-CEO made my hands clammy. But I'd never fallen short of grit, and now wasn't the time to leave my involvement in the ranch to chance.

Maggie opened the cupboard door and took out three ice cream dishes without saying a word. I appreciated her sensitivity even though her forehead was pinched. She opened the freezer while Dad loaded the dishes into the washer. Something he didn't usually do.

"What are you doing?" I asked.

"Helping. You want to take on more responsibility with the ranch, maybe I should add a little something extra from this end."

Maggie approved and scooped the huckleberry ice cream. Her favorite dessert. "Chloe, can you put this carton away for me, please?"

The frost on the carton bit my fingertips. The container slipped out of my hands and hit the floor. Maggie and I bent down at the same time to grab it. Our heads clunked together. "Not quite a cracker box," I said, rubbing the sting away.

"Again, an unforgettable day." Maggie giggled.

I may have been seven, but I was savvy. Dad and I had moved in next door to Maggie. She and Dad didn't exactly get along at first. So I had gone on a mission to make friends because Maggie needed one. And the rest became the story of us.

"Remember when I took the stitches out?" Dad touched Maggie's temple.

"Of course I do. Having a neighbor who was a doctor had its perks. Lucky for me, you didn't return to your daddy's ranch before practicing pediatrics in Michigan," Maggie said with a smile.

"And I kissed you," Dad said.

Maggie blushed. She dipped her spoon into one of the dishes of ice cream, nibbled the bite away, then licked the spoon clean. Her cheeks puckered. "So good."

Dad laughed, and she swatted him with the dish towel. He scooted out of her reach before she could get him again.

"It's been another fine day, I'd say." She put the lid on the carton. "Put this away before I want seconds. I gained so much weight when I was pregnant with Bradley. Don't want to go there again."

"That was forty-one years ago. So dramatic," I said.

Bradley, my stepbrother, lived in Boston and favored his mom in many ways. My stomach flopped at the thought of gaining weight. If there was one thing I wanted from my mom, it was her figure.

"When Mom was pregnant with me, did she

gain a lot of weight?" I asked Dad.

Dad frowned. "This conversation has taken a precarious turn," he said. "I'm not sure, but I *am* sure discussing a woman's weight never ends well."

I dipped a spoon into my ice cream. "Like you need to worry with your size-six jeans," I said.

"Hey, hey. Gravity and time are *not* a woman's friend." Maggie savored her dessert like it was the last bowl of huckleberry ice cream on earth.

"You look great," Dad said.

"You two are so weird," I joked.

"We know," they said in unison.

"How did you not find each other from the get-go?"

Dad and Maggie even shrugged in unison.

"Guess somebody else had different plans for us. All that matters is that we're together now," Maggie said.

Dad took the dish towel from the counter and snapped it in her direction. She held her bowl of ice cream close to her chest. Dad leaned over and kissed her forehead, then he stepped closer to me, touched my temple, and kissed me, too.

"Gotta love hardheaded women." He put the ice cream back in the fridge. "Better put this away before it melts."

"Like my heart." Maggie batted her eyelashes.

I leaned against the counter. I couldn't picture Maggie pregnant and out of shape like she always says she was. I licked my lips and stuck my spoon back in the bowl. "You really gonna hire another guy?"

"We need one. You said it yourself," Dad said. "Matt won't be with us indefinitely."

How long would he stick around, especially now? How would I work the land and be taken seriously with a baby bump?

"I'll be in the office if anyone needs me." Dad tossed the dish towel on the counter.

Maggie rinsed out her sticky dish and put it in the dishwasher. She leaned into me. My nerves prickled.

"When you want to talk about Matt, I'm here," she whispered.

"Everything's cool. No worries." I put my empty dish in the dishwasher, too. I cleared my throat and stuffed my hands in my pockets. "Thanks, Maggie." The glint in her eyes reminded me of Grandpa when he knew my insides were knotted like old rope and my heart had been trampled like a cowboy beneath a cantankerous bull.

"You're welcome, Chloe. You know I love you."

"I know. I just wanted to say thank you. I know I've been a handful and still am most days."

"What child isn't at times?" She paused. "But you're not a child anymore. You're a grown woman."

I swallowed the tension building at the back of my throat.

"Chloe—"

Her hand rested on my forearm. Shivers danced down my spine.

"What, Maggie?"

"Nothing," she said. "I'll leave it alone. You'll tell me when you're ready."

I wanted this to be the end of the conversation. I wanted to be up on the mountain, but the sky was dark, and the horses were done for the day. Dad poked his head back into the kitchen.

"When you two are done chatting, could I borrow you, Maggie?"

"Sure," she said.

The hair on my arm bristled. "Go ahead. I should check the barn."

"You sure?" she asked.

"I'm sure. You two have fun making out," I teased. Maggie blushed, and I laughed. Dad rolled his eyes at me. "Be back soon." I clicked my tongue against the roof of my mouth. My insides tingled with fever to flee.

CHAPTER 3

I SHUT THE mudroom door and welcomed the cool evening breeze. I meandered next to the creek and over the footbridge. The glow in the barn trickled into the Montana night air like soft words asking me for the first dance.

I leaned against the fence and rested my chin on clasped hands, staring into the umbrella of darkness. The sound of horse hooves thundered across the pasture. Sunny's nose grazed mine as she came to a halt.

"Watcha doing, girl?" I nuzzled close. Her whiskers brushed my cheek. "When I came to this place, you were a spunky filly. You used to chase me around the pond." I dug in my pocket and pulled out two sugar cubes. "I'll always have treats." Her soft lips tickled my palm.

"What am I going to do?" She pawed at the ground with her front hoof. "I know," I said. She nudged me. Her soft breath warmed my neck.

"You were always so good with her."

I turned toward the sound of Trout's voice.

"Sorry, didn't mean to startle you. Everything okay?"

"Everything's fine," I said. "Sunny likes it when I talk to her."

"She adores you. Always has. You've got the makings of a fine rancher."

"Thanks."

"You always have, kid." Trout leaned against the fence. "That's a long face for someone with big plans. If you've got something stuck in your craw, you best bring it up with your daddy directly."

"He's hiring another hand. I put my two cents in, but when I mentioned being co-CEO, he pulled in the reins."

Trout inhaled a drag from his cigarette. The red glow lit the dim space between us. "When your granddaddy made your daddy co-CEO, he figured it was the one way to keep his son here after years of chasing a city career. Your daddy had already run off, made a name for himself—"

"Had a shotgun wedding and a baby."

Smoke streamed through Trout's nostrils. "Yes, he'd married your mother and had you." He sighed. "You're on a different path than your daddy. Nothing 'bout you says you're strayin'. And your daddy doesn't need any reminders he's getting older." He took another drag from his cigarette.

Thinking about inheriting this ranch was inevitable. Thinking about Dad aging, unfathomable.

"Kid, there's always something to learn. You got time. Unless you got something better to do," he said.

The urge to run this place had crept into my blood when I first moved here and rooted itself deep in my dreams. "I do have a standing offer with Dr. Neely in Bozeman. She says she'll hire me on to work with the animals."

"I remember your first day here." Trout chuckled. "Rustling up the barn cat, kicking your feet in the dirt, pouting about leaving your friends, and moaning about your dad dragging you from place to place. You don't want to work at vet Neely's, and you know it."

"The cat's name was French Fry." I rested my foot on the bottom rail of the fence. "I'm still upset with him for dying on me. Thought he'd live forever. Kind of like Grandpa." Trout's expression went solemn. "Sorry. I shouldn't have said that."

"Don't be sorry. He was the best friend I ever had."

"I think you miss him as much as I do, some days more." The moon peeked out from behind a silver cloud. "Maggie says he's still here."

Trout dropped his cigarette butt into the dirt, stomped it out with the toe of his boot, then reached down to retrieve it. His knees cracked, and the crickets answered with a serenade.

"Do you think he's here?" I asked.

"He's hanging around somewhere. That old coot couldn't leave this place anymore than you could. Those cattle called to him day in and day out. Some days, I swear I get a glimpse of old Winston from the corner of my eye when I'm wrangling." The darkening sky masked his stare.

I imagined Grandpa on his horse, brawny and tall and strong. "Maggie's probably right. She usually is."

Trout chuckled and shook his head.

"What?" I asked.

"Maggie's one strong woman. She could give your grandma, Ida May, a run for her money."

"Dad says we're hardheaded."

Trout slapped his gloves against his thigh, then tucked them in his back pocket.

"We're not *too* hardheaded, are we?" I followed him into the barn. The aroma of leather, fresh hay, hard work, and love for this place lingered in the air. Tack lined the walls in neat rows. Rough timber, clean as ever, soaked up the dim light.

"No. Just the right amount to feed your determination."

I sat on the tack box near the far end of the barn, my back rested against the wall. I touched the worn leather bridle straps next to me. I imagined Grandpa's arms around me, holding me close in the Montana night by an open fire. My cheeks warmed at the thought of the glowing embers. "I wish I would've known my grandma," I said.

Trout put his saddle on an empty peg, then secured it. "Ida May was something," he said. "She would've loved having you around. Your sass reminds me of her. She never took a back seat to nobody. I'm sorry you never met her, kid, but somehow, someday you'll know. All roads lead home."

I studied the lines in Trout's face. He was family, a hard worker, and tough as nails. Grandpa did the right thing making him foreman and letting him live in the old house down by the river.

"That's what Maggie says, too. My road led here." Dad knew Montana was in my blood before I did.

"Guess so," Trout said. "You gonna turn out the light when you're done?"

"Yes." I picked at the fray in my jeans, basking

in the stillness.

"Good girl." Trout closed the office door. "Night, darlin'." His footsteps faded into the distance.

I pulled the navy bandana from my vest pocket, tied it around my head, knotted the ends, then pushed the edge back from my forehead. I leaned against the wall and closed my eyes. I took deep breaths, trying to settle the truths gnawing at me.

The sound of Matt's familiar gait neared, and I peeked through narrow slits. Hoping to be invisible, I pulled my knees close to my chest as his gaze met mine.

"Hey. I thought Trout was out here milling around," he said.

"He was. He left. What do you need him for?"

Matt hooked his thumbs in his back pockets. His fleece-lined plaid shirt was worn thin at the elbows, and his jeans were smudged with mud. "Just planning a fishing trip. He's gonna teach me how to fish."

I wrinkled my forehead at him. "You already know how to fish."

"I'm an amateur when it comes to tying flies and strategy. He's a master."

"You're silly." I stopped laughing when Matt sat next to me.

"Maybe, but at least I'll admit it," he said.

"What's that supposed to mean?"

Matt took off his hat and ran his fingers through his thick, dark hair. "Nothing."

He rested his hand on my knee. The warmth from his touch penetrated the denim. I let go of my legs and planted my feet on the floor. Coal, the black barn cat, ran across my boots.

"That cat is always chasing something," I said.

"No different than people, I suppose. She darts around here like there's something hiding around every corner. Sometimes, it's just a corner." Matt brushed dust from his shirt, then wiped his forehead with a bandana.

Coal stopped at the stall door closest to me. Her green eyes glistened as she stalked in the shadows. "Come here, pretty girl." I patted my thigh. She leaped over Matt and into my lap. I stroked her arched back until she curled up and purred.

"Dang, wish I had your charm."

Was he kidding? "You're plenty charming." I swallowed the secret creeping up the back of my throat.

"Really? Those sound like words of interest. Thought you wanted to stick to the friends with benefits kind of relationship."

"I think it's best." The words stung. We'd be linked for life. That one time we'd been together, let down our guards, was no longer the memory of a spontaneous tryst on a perfect summer Montana day.

"I wish—" he breathed out.

I couldn't tell him about the baby before I came to terms with the pregnancy. How could I tell him we were going to become parents when I'd always said I didn't want marriage or children? Coal jumped from my lap and ran away. "What do you wish?"

"Nothing. There's no sense in arguing about it."

My shoulders tensed. The spark floating between us faded.

Matt and I weren't meant to be.

CHAPTER 4

THE DAWN BROUGHT an electric energy I couldn't explain. The sleepless night hadn't depleted me like I thought it would have. I'd gotten up before the sun, helped run the horses, done my chores, gotten the word out that we were hiring, and eaten lunch. Staying busy would help me sort out my feelings, keep my mind moving forward, and focus on how to become Dad's co-CEO.

Light filtered through the trees like golden drops of hope. With my hat pulled down, I lowered my head and let Gypsy pick the route to the top of the mountain. Her instincts and sure-footedness balanced my impulsivity.

Her short strides navigated the roots and rocks up the narrow path. Shaggy pines brushed my shoulders. Ground cover and towering trees disguised the altitude. Sweat trickled down my back. Which was ironic because Gypsy carried the load.

Sun poured over us as we made our way across the ridge of sage and wildflowers. Gypsy's sepia coat speckled with black hair shimmered when she craned her neck to see me.

We both knew we'd arrived at our desired destination.

For her, it was a field of wonderful and beautiful things to graze on, and for me it was my sacred place, a field of peace and sanctuary.

"We don't need words here, do we, girl?"

She shook her head; her black mane tickled my knuckles. I loved Gypsy as much as Dad adored her mother, Breeze. She dipped her head and yanked the reins.

"Just as beautiful, without the wild streak. And faster." Gypsy sniffed the yellow forget-me-nots near her feet.

"Come on, girl." I nudged her with my heels after she snatched a mouthful of groundcover. She nibbled the green blades of grass hanging from her mouth until they were gone. She knew the way.

"I remember the day you were born. I was fifteen. We were all there when Grandpa helped you into the world. I love you, girl." Babies should know they're loved every day, not just on special occasions.

At the edge of the ridge, I spotted the yellow rose bush marking Grandpa's memorial and the place where we scattered his ashes. Dad had said miners used to plant rose bushes to mark the gold they'd found. Grandpa was McIntyre gold.

Some days I missed him worse than others, like today. I pulled back and Gypsy slowed up. "I'm getting off here, girl." I swung my leg over the rear of the saddle and lowered myself carefully until my feet touched the ground. I led her to a shady spot, then tied her to a pine. Her brown eyes followed me until I undid the saddlebag and pulled out a juicy apple. Her whiskers twitched, and she ate it from my palm.

I reached into the other saddlebag to retrieve a jug of water. I walked toward the stone cross next to the rosebush. The tall grass brushed against my shins. I whispered each letter of Grandpa's name as my finger stroked the coarse stone. Winston Ludlow McIntyre.

I unscrewed the cap and drained the jug at the base of the plant covered in yellow blooms. Dad and Maggie did their best to keep the bush groomed. Their knowledge for plants exceeded mine, and they knew I'd be crushed if it withered away.

Today, I thought I'd do my best to follow in their footsteps. I had to begin somewhere. I picked off the shriveled leaves and dead twigs. I jerked my hand back at the sound of horse hooves coming across the ridge. A thorn caught the edge of my thumb, and I flinched. I licked the trickle of blood, then sucked my finger clean.

Maggie rode like a champ. Mom may have donned countless magazine pages with her poise and confidence, but Maggie owned the mountain.

From the day she came to visit the ranch, she'd been a natural in the saddle. Her strawberry blond braid trailed down her back. She loved Montana as much as she loved my dad.

I screwed the lid back onto the empty jug and watched her. With a hand on her hip, she sunk farther into Cora's saddle, then checked the position of the sun.

"Hey, what are you doing up here?" I asked.

She searched her saddlebag and pulled out a radio. "You forgot this."

I checked my belt. Taking a radio was the rule, and I had forgotten it like so many other things along the way, such as the consequences of having sex, even if Matt and I had taken precautions.

I took the radio from her. "Sorry," I said.

That was Maggie, always looking out for others. God knew what He was doing when this woman married my dad and raised me as her own.

"Sure is hot today." She took the bandana from her shirt pocket and wiped her brow.

"Sure is," I said, watching Gypsy snooze.

Maggie leaned forward, rested her left hand on the horn of the saddle, and patted Cora's neck with the other hand. Her sandy-brown mane reminded me of the Michigan beach where we used to swim.

"What's the smile for?" Maggie asked.

"I was thinking about our beach."

"We had a lot of good times there and some not-so-good ones, too."

"I prefer the good ones."

Maggie stood in her stirrups, then swung her left leg over the back of her saddle to dismount. "Me too," she said as her toes found solid ground.

"You shrinking?" I inspected her stance.

"Hope not. I'd like to think I'm still taller than my mom," she answered.

"Um, I hate to break it to you, but she's a lot shorter than she used to be."

Maggie chuckled. "It's all relative. You've been taller than me since seventh grade."

Seventh grade seemed like ages ago. All that mattered back then was the rodeo and riding. I couldn't enter enough competitions. Trophies and ribbons lined the bookshelves in my bedroom.

Maggie's radio crackled. She plucked it from her belt and adjusted the volume to answer Dad.

"Yes, she's up here. No worries. I'll let you know when we're coming back down."

I peered into the valley at the White Park cattle. From the ridge, they resembled white dots the size of cotton balls. Grandpa had cultivated the eccentric herd, and Dad was keeping Grandpa's labor of love alive. I breathed in the sweet Montana air.

"Sorry I made an extra trip for you, but thanks. I should've checked my gear." I should have known better about lots of things. She raised an eyebrow at me with a knowing glint.

Maggie led Cora into the shade and tied her next to Gypsy. Cora kicked at the ground, then settled down. When Maggie noticed the empty jug, she smiled. "You came up here to water the roses?"

"Yep," I said, rubbing the back of my neck.

Maggie put her hands in the back pockets of her worn blue jeans. "I get the shivers when I think about how much work your grandfather put into this ranch." Her cowboy hat threw a shadow across her shoulders but not a big enough one to cut the day's unexpected heat. "You're a good woman, Chloe Jean."

"Great, you're middle-naming me. I wish I had my grandma's middle name. What do you think of

Chloe May?"

"You could change it."

"We'll see. It'd hurt my mom's feelings if I did. And besides, Jean is your middle name, too. I'd like to believe I have a little of you in my gene pool."

Maggie kneeled beside the rose bush and inspected the buttery petals of the blooms. "When are you going to tell your dad you're pregnant?" She touched the stone cross with Grandpa's name on it and stood.

"I should have remembered the radio."

"I'm not going to say anything to your dad or anyone else. That's up to you." She caressed my cheek. "I'm here if you need me."

I gave the hard dirt a swift kick. Tiny pebbles shot over the rocky ridge. How had she become so caring? Would I be as patient or insightful when it came to raising a child?

My chin quivered, and I wiped my forehead with the back of my hand. Maggie wrapped her arms around me, our hat brims knocking together. Maggie pushed loose strands of hair from my cheeks.

"How did you know?"

"Matt said you were acting funny. Dinner. The pregnancy test in the garbage."

"I bet Bradley never got away with anything."

"I'm sure he got away with plenty, but this isn't about him. It's about you. Matt doesn't know, does he?"

I peered at her from beneath my lashes. "No, and I don't want to tell him."

"You'll have to tell him whether you want to or not."

"I didn't want this." I rested my head on her shoulder when she draped her arm around me. "How come you're not lecturing me? I thought you'd be disappointed."

"Lecturing won't do any good."

"What am I gonna do?" I held her stare.

"I don't know," Maggie said. "It's not up to me."

CHAPTER 5

I STOOD ON a log, preparing to mount Gypsy, and Maggie stopped me.

"No rough riding," she said.

I hesitated before swinging my leg over the saddle that used to be my grandpa's. I bore down, clenching the horn. "I'll be fine. Pregnant women can still ride." The worn leather was cool beneath my britches even with the rising temperature.

She led Cora to the middle of the field by the big stone to mount her horse. I appreciated her ingenuity. I tugged at the front of my hat, and Gypsy swished her tail as we dallied.

"Cora's coat matches your hair," I said.

Maggie smiled and set her feet in the stirrups and settled in for the ride home. She nudged Cora with her heels and circled me like a dutiful cattle dog.

"I mean it. No crazy riding." Her words were loud and clear, as if she were rounding up strays.

"All right." We rode side by side across the field, our horses in stride. Taming my riding habits would take as much effort as taming my attitude.

"Maggie?"

"Yeah," she said, resting her hand on her thigh.

"Thanks for caring so much."

She tugged at the front of her hat as we neared the pines. "You're welcome. We've been through a lot together. It's the least I can do."

Cora slowed her pace on the narrow path through the trees. Reddish-blond strands of hair strayed from Maggie's braid. She glanced back over taut shoulders.

"How do you think Dad's going to react?"

Maggie shrugged.

"That good, huh. Thought parents lived for grandbabies."

Maggie's forehead creased.

"Sorry, just trying to be funny." Truth was, I'd been weighing my options about keeping the baby. But I'd keep those thoughts to myself. Talking to Matt came first.

I scanned the terrain as we rode down the mountain. Bristly pine needles scratched my skin, then a tree branch caught my arm. Neither hurt as much as the truth about being pregnant. "I should've worn long sleeves. The trees are out to get me today."

Maggie put her right hand on Cora's hindquarters and leaned back. "This is pretty huge."

"Thanks for the reminder. Life as I know it will be over."

"I wouldn't say it's going to be over, but things will certainly be different."

"No, I'm pretty sure it'll be over. In my opinion, having children is like careening through a ditch. You have to hold on and hope for the best," I said. "I didn't think I'd ever have children. I prefer four-legged friends. I have no business having a baby."

"Why?" Maggie lowered her gaze to the path ahead.

"Because I'm my mother's daughter. Have you met me?" I paused. "Animals, I can handle. I'm pretty sure Mom prefers animals to children, too. Probably one of the few things we have in common." I fingered the heart charm on the silver necklace my mom had given me when I was eight. I'd worn it nearly everyday. Wished on it. And sworn on it. I held it tightly in the palm of my hand.

Maggie's dimpled profile appreciated my sarcasm.

The bushes rustled, and we stopped as two deer leaped through the foliage. Their white tails bobbed, then disappeared into the dense forest.

"You do keep things lively," she said.

"I want you to know, we weren't careless. I'm not sure how this happened." I fanned my warm cheeks. "I mean…I *know* how it happened. I don't know why the birth control failed." I fiddled with the reins. "I'm not very good at talking about private matters."

"You're doing fine," Maggie said. "You ready to move on?"

"Yes, let's get going." Cora stepped around a patch of rock poking through the earth at the top of the ridge. I gave Gypsy a nudge when Maggie got to the bottom.

My body swayed with Gypsy's movements. Gnarled tree roots impeded swift strides and hasty decisions. Flecks of sunlight glittered through the trees. With the reins loose in one hand, I wrapped my fingers through Gypsy's mane and held tightly. I praised her as she took me safely down the mountainside.

Cora flicked her tail and pawed at the ground, beckoning us to move faster. "We're coming, Cora," I called.

"Your dad thinks it's funny when I talk to the horses."

"There's not an animal I don't talk to on this ranch. You gotta talk to them. And don't let Dad fool you. He talks to them plenty."

We rode single file through the next stretch of grassy flat land. Maggie stopped before the next descent. Her gaze searched my face.

"What?" I asked.

She leaned back in her saddle and supported her weight with one hand on Cora's rump. "I'm not sure I should say it."

"You might as well. I probably need to hear it all before I talk to Dad." I anticipated a whole lot of whisker rubbing, a barrage of questions, and an agenda of how I was going to handle the situation.

"You must be nervous." Maggie pushed her hat back from her forehead, her concern unveiled.

I loosened my grip on the reins. "I am," I said. I leaned on the saddle horn with both hands. "I'm not married and wasn't planning on it." Most women I knew craved children and building a family. But I craved the independence to change my mind when I wanted to follow whatever interested me until it didn't, and to focus on what I deemed important in my life without taking responsibility for someone else's life too. "Being single and living my best life was all I wanted." I let this truth settle. "I've never said that out loud before."

A haunting bellow came from the shadows.

Cora and Gypsy's ears perked up at the warning. The hairs on the back of my neck bristled.

Maggie pointed to a momma moose protecting her baby. Cora jumped at the sight, then trotted ahead. Gypsy danced sideways across the rocky path, scattering dark pieces of shale.

"Come on, girl, let's go." Gypsy scraped the ground with her front hoof then trotted off. I fell in line with her strides for a smooth ride until we caught up to Maggie.

"Did you see the calf?" she asked.

"Yep," I said, checking behind me. My heart raced at the thought of being charged.

"You okay?" Maggie asked.

I nodded.

"Just be careful."

"I was, and look where being careful got me," I announced as Gypsy jerked the reins so she could sniff the tall grass in the last field before we were back home.

SAMSON GREETED US at the barn with a woof. He waddled into the pasture; his tongue waggled from his jowls.

I dismounted, shook out my legs, and unbuckled the girth. Gypsy's slick hide was damp to the touch. The saddle slid from her back, and I fumbled to catch it.

Matt hustled over to help me.

"Thanks." I dried the palms of my hands on my jeans.

"Anytime." He took the saddle to the barn.

I caught Maggie's stare, slipped the bridle over Gypsy's head, and followed Matt. He whistled a country tune to his easy stride and hoisted my tack to the peg where I kept it. I'd carved my name in the wood when I was twelve. My mark was still there.

At the time, Dad had told me not to. And of course, I couldn't help myself.

Knots of uncertainty filled my belly. How long could I keep the pregnancy from Matt? How long into the pregnancy could I ride? If I had my way, I'd be on a horse until the due date.

"Have you been out fixing ditches again?" I pointed to Matt's muddy boot heels.

"Uh-huh. Seems like I'm always fixing ditches." He straightened the fleecy woolen pad beneath Grandpa's saddle.

I detected a hint of Grandpa's musky after-shave—a lingering treasure.

I thought he'd live forever. Guess forever seems like a mighty long time when you're young. A breeze billowed through the barn door, and a shiver swept down my spine. Matt's hat fell to the ground, and we both reached for it. He picked it up and brushed off the dust. His brown eyes shimmered in the light.

"You've been acting kind of funny, Chloe."

"What do you mean?" I pulled back and hooked my fingers through my belt loops.

"I thought things were good between us. Did I do something to upset you?"

I balked at his question, remembering how his skin felt against mine. I scuffled over to the tack box and hung Gypsy's bridle next to the door. "No."

"Then what gives? You've been quiet, and you're never quiet." Matt put his hat back on.

"I have a lot on my mind," I said.

"Me too." He planted his hands on his hips. He was a fine specimen for a cowboy, but not in a flashy sense. His strong jaw, kind nature, and backbone solidified his sense of integrity and work ethic. "Someday, I'll have my own ranch. I've got big plans."

Nerves prickled my skin. I had the same plan. But being parents meant a shift in priorities.

His left dimple tugged at my heart. "What's on your mind, Chloe?"

Matt stepped closer. I braced myself on the doorjamb. He reached over me, planted his hand above my head, and leaned in. My heart buckled. Emotion caught at the back of my throat.

"Not sure you'd understand," I said.

"Not understand? Chloe, we spend more time together than most siblings. Nothing like selling me short."

He shifted his weight, and I sidestepped the unexpected electricity.

"What are you doing?" I asked.

"Reminding you that there's nothing you can't tell me."

I rested my hands on my hips. My mind reeled. "I'm scared." The words were a relief.

"Scared of what? You're the fiercest woman I know."

"A baby."

"Chloe, what do babies have to do with riding and wrangling?"

"*We're* having a baby, Matt."

"What?"

"I'm pregnant. And you're the father."

"How?" His brows dipped. "We used birth control."

I shrugged. "I don't know." I peered over his shoulder into the corral where the horses grazed.

"Look at me," Matt said. "Are you sure?"

"The pregnancy test I took was positive."

"Maybe you should do it again."

I half-heartedly chuckled. "I did. Seven times." I looked him square in the eye. "They were positive—*all seven of them.*" My hands fell from my hips.

Matt stood speechless. He rubbed his chin the way I thought my dad would when I told him the news, too.

"Who knows besides us?" he asked.

"Maggie," I answered. "She said she wouldn't tell Dad or anyone else."

Matt tossed his hat on the tack box. He massaged his temples and paced. I waited for him to say something. He covered his face with his hands and shook his head. He peeked through his fingers. "You sure you took the test right?"

"This was one test I didn't need to study for. It wasn't too difficult to pee on a stick and wait for the results. Except, I have to say, waiting for the results was nerve-wracking."

"Are you going to the doctor to make sure?" He continued pacing like a nervous mountain cat.

"I already did. The doctor confirmed it. My next appointment with the obstetrician is next week. Dr. Hennessey said she'd like to meet you."

Coal rubbed against my leg. I bent down to scratch her ears.

Matt mumbled under his breath while running his hands through his hair, his glazed response like a deer in the headlights.

"And by the way, you're not making me feel better about our situation." I walked out of the barn, leaned against the fence rail, bowed my head on clasped hands, and said a prayer.

Matt rested his hand on the back of my neck. He didn't say anything.

"I'm sorry." The words caught in my throat.

Matt's hand found my stomach. I laced my fingers with his and forced myself to look him in the eye. His radio screeched with blurred static, then my dad's voice interrupted. Matt pulled the radio from the back of his belt.

"Yeah, I'm here," he answered.

The pines dotting the mountainside held my attention. I pictured my grandmother's face among the soft clouds rolling in. *Trout says I have your sass. Something tells me I know you better than I think. Stay with me, Grandma.*

"I'll be right there, John." Matt signed off and hooked the radio back on his belt. "And I'll be there next week when you see the obstetrician. We'll figure this out, Chloe. I promise. But right now, they need an extra hand with the cattle. Got some rowdy calves." He hustled out of the other end of the barn.

"I can help." I followed on his heels. He grabbed his saddle horn, hoisted himself up, and swung his leg over the back of his chestnut speckled horse, Trigger, who showed me his teeth on cue. I fed him a sugar cube from my pocket and patted his snout.

"No worries. I've got your back. Hopefully, we'll have an extra hand soon."

"You've always had my back. Something would go wrong at school and you were there. Something broke, you were my go-to man. I could always count on you."

"Still can. We'll talk later. You stay put and get Gypsy cleaned up. I won't be long." Matt nudged Trigger with his heels and rode off.

Gypsy stood near the hitching post, her eyelids at half-mast. I clicked my tongue and untied her lead. We made our way into the barn, our heavy steps in unison. I'd read about being tired while pregnant, and I was starting to feel it.

Maggie hobbled past me.

"Did you hurt yourself?" I asked.

"I fell off Cora. I'm gonna *really* feel it tomorrow." She kneaded her tailbone.

"What happened?"

"I was helping with the cattle. I stopped to dismount, and when I swung my leg over, Cora got spooked. I tripped and landed on my rear end. Nothing major, but major enough to remind me I'm not getting any younger. My pride's more bruised than my behind."

"You gonna tell Dad you're hurt?"

"I'll see how I feel tomorrow." She sat on the tack box.

"It's hard for you, isn't it?" I patted Gypsy's thick rump.

Maggie brushed off her pants. "What do you mean?"

"Admitting when you hurt." I took the pick from my back pocket and lifted Gypsy's back foot. Maggie didn't answer. I stopped what I was doing and looked up at her. "I told Matt."

"I saw."

I finished grooming Gypsy and put her in the corral. Shards of sunlight pierced the gray sky and rained down, showering me with hope. I shaded my eyes and smiled at Ida May's offering.

CHAPTER 6

THE VINTAGE PICKUP bumped along the dirt road. Matt drove, his arm propped in the open window, his attention focused on the horizon ahead.

I stared out the window and tried to picture my life with a child. Dad had done a fine job raising me by himself for most my life. He got over his fear of buying me tampons, and I learned how to interpret his stoic emotions.

I'd met plenty of people who didn't have the support I had growing up. I'd met plenty of people who did and more. And if someone asked me today, I'd say I was right where I needed to be. The only forks in the road were the ones I'd created.

Matt had been left on his parents' doorstep, neatly tucked inside a plastic laundry bin, a note pinned to his blanket. He'd been discarded without a voice and lucky enough to be left with caring people who made him their own. Our stories were so different yet formulated from a common thread. We understood each other. Our friendship was based on trust and reliability.

Shivers ran down my spine at the sight of the white cattle basking in the sun. They were strong and robust, a breed cultivated across the pond. Their horns grew toward the light like hands reaching for heaven.

Matt stopped the truck, opened his door, and jumped out. I put on my cowboy hat and reached for the handle. My gaze met his through the open window. "You keep your distance from the cattle," he said.

"Whatever," I sputtered. Clearly, my condition had become a hazardous impediment. "I've been around them pretty much all my life. I know what to do out here."

"Please, stay out of the way. I don't want you getting hurt."

"Seriously? I won't be a sideline participant when it comes to this ranch." Matt's caution didn't soften my disposition. "I'm getting out of this truck one way or another."

He opened the squeaky passenger door.

"The hinges could use some oil," I said. The scent of sweet morning dew lingered in the air. He touched my arm.

"Things are different now."

I shaded my eyes and scanned the grassy pasture. "I know, but I still have to be me. And being me means wrangling cattle, riding, and ranching."

"I know. All I'm saying is, be careful."

"I'm not out there chasing bulls or riding today. This is stressful enough. Please don't coddle me. Or make me feel like I'm doing something wrong, because I'm not."

Matt lowered his voice. "This baby is part of both of us. And I care about your safety. I'll do my best not to *coddle* you if you'll do your best not to dismiss me when I show concern."

The energy between us bristled my independence.

Justin rode up on a dappled gray horse. He'd hired on ten years ago. He seemed more like a brother than a hired hand. His wit and friendship made him easy to like. I envied his slow pace when it came to learning and enjoying life. I scrunched up my nose at him. "Well, look who the cat dragged in. Do we get you for the rest of the summer?"

"Sure do. What's left of it. I'll be here on the weekends until the homework takes over. Being out here beats studying in a library under artificial light. I've left the basics in the bunkhouse, and the rest of my things are at school. It'll make going back and forth easier."

"What's your horse's name, and where'd you get her?" Her withers glistened from work. I pulled some sugar from my pocket; her brown gaze watched my every move.

"This is Belle. She's my new girl. Had my eye on her for some time before I could afford her." The apples of his cheeks ballooned with pride. "Don't spoil her too much with that sugar of yours, now."

Belle swished her tail as she shifted her weight. I noticed Matt tug at the front of his hat and frown. "You're a beauty," I said, stroking Belle's face. I squinted into the sun to get a better look at Justin. He appeared broad-chested and taller in the saddle. Justin's stature had matured over the summer.

An unknown rider appeared on the horizon. "Who's that?"

"That's my brother, Tristan. He drove in last night with his two horses."

Tristan's tall, thin frame moved in time with his horse's canter. With the sunlight at his back, I couldn't see his face. He wore a large, flat-brimmed hat. His coffee-colored horse with spotted hindquarters eased up as he neared. Dad rode alongside him.

"This is my daughter, Chloe," Dad said.

Tristan nodded. "I've heard a lot about you," he said.

"Oh boy." I tucked my hands in my back pockets. I hadn't heard anything about him.

"All good things," Tristan added. "I'm sure I'll be seeing you later." He tipped his hat and rode off. Justin followed.

"Before you say anything. I haven't hired him on yet. He's gonna spend some time here to see if he's a good fit," Dad said.

"Interesting—I thought you would've told me he was joining us. What gives? We've got other interviews scheduled, and I don't recall Tristan being on the list."

A bull meandered in our direction, his deep bellow a welcome greeting. Matt stepped closer to me. The sweet gesture ruffled my nerves. Obviously, we'd revisit our conversation. He raised his brow. My palms sweated with the prickly heat between us. He sure was taking this pregnancy to heart.

"Simmer down, now. Justin mentioned Tristan was looking for work. Word of mouth is sometimes better than a written resumé. Matt seems to think he's a fine candidate for the job." Dad said.

Dad had a point, but he was missing mine. He and Matt discussed the prospects of taking on

Tristan without me. And since when did Matt get a voice in the matter? The limitless boundaries of the wide-open land closed in on me. "I get a vote, right?" Until now, I'd felt like one of the guys.

Dad's sigh didn't hide his feelings. "Nothing has been decided. I promise we'll discuss hiring him together. And from my perspective, having him ride with us is the best interview process I can think of." Dad tugged on the brim of his hat and nudged Breeze. Her hooves thudded against the earth, then trailed off as they rode away.

The curious bull, still in my line of vision, batted his tail to and fro like a pendulum at midnight while grazing at a snail's pace.

"Dang, girl. What was that all about?" Matt asked.

"Business," I answered.

Tristan rode over. "This bull's been straggling all morning. Sure is poky." Tristan shifted his weight in his saddle.

"He's just saying hello," I said. "What's your horse's name?"

"Hitch. Short for Hitchcock, Texas. His hometown. My other ride is back at the ranch. Have you met Casanova?"

"Not yet," I answered, letting Hitch sniff my fingers.

"He tends to be cautious around new people. He seems to like you."

Hitch found my pocket. "Can he have some sugar?" I stroked his nose, waiting for permission.

"I guess," he said. "He doesn't get many treats."

I fed him the sugar. "I like your white star and blue eyes." I let my fingers trail down Hitch's neck to his shoulder. "Pretty horse."

"Won him in a bet," Tristan said.

I frowned.

"Don't worry, I got him fair and square," he reassured me. "We really should be moving on." With a flick of the reins, he rode away. The bull trotted behind.

"He's got another horse here? Sounds like he's staying," I said.

"Relax. Your dad's got it covered."

"He said we'd go through this process together. I've scheduled interviews with the wranglers Dad thought had potential, and this guy shows up unannounced."

Matt and I walked back to the truck. He popped the hood and jiggled the wires. "What's the matter?" I pretended to understand the engine I was inspecting.

"With the truck or your attitude?" He stuck his

fingers into a narrow crevice of the engine, then winced. "Darn this thing."

"The truck, of course." I leaned against the fender. "You'd totally stick up for yourself if you were in my position. Dad and I talked about hiring someone together. This is not together. Tristan Donoghue shows up, and I know nothing about it."

"Suppose so." Matt wiped his hands on his jeans, his cross expression an invitation.

"You know you would," I said.

"All I'm sayin' is, give it some time. Everyone around here isn't on your clock." Matt shut the hood.

"Well, my clock isn't ticking any slower now that we're expecting." I slid into the passenger seat and buckled up.

Matt settled into the driver's seat and turned the key in the ignition. The engine idled. He faced me and leaned closer. "Focus, Chloe."

"I *am* focused." I took my hat off and tied a bandana around my head. I replayed the scene. We drove out to the field. We had words about my safety. Justin and Dad rode up. We met Tristan. He returned to round up the strays. I fed his horse sugar. "What did I do?"

Matt shifted the truck into gear, cranked the

wheel, and revved the engine.

"What's wrong?"

"You're pregnant, and I'm the father. You've made it clear you'll be calling the shots with your health and our situation. Not to mention, all the shots alongside your dad. You're going overboard." His temple twitched like my father's when his fuse ran short. "This baby is taking a toll on us already, and we haven't even told your dad yet." He let up on the gas. "I thought the drive together would be nice. Thought maybe we could talk. Guess not."

"Stop the truck!" I unbuckled and covered my mouth.

Matt slammed on the brakes. I pushed the door open, leaned over the running board, and vomited. He got out and hurried to console me. I threw up two more times. My eyes stung, and a rancid taste filled my mouth. He pushed hair away from my face, then handed me the bandana from his back pocket.

"I'm sorry," he said.

I wiped my face clean and caught my breath. "For what?"

"For everything." He poked his hat away from his brow and rubbed his chin. "Let's get you back to the house."

"Please don't say you're sorry. I don't want your pity, Matt."

"This isn't pity, woman. What I feel runs a lot deeper."

CHAPTER 7

A N UNEXPECTED CHILL crept across the valley as night rolled in, the dusky air stagnant. The smoky ribbon drifting toward me promised another cozy fire and fellowship. With autumn upon us, our nightly gatherings around the firepit would wane until spring brought promising weather. I shoved my hands into the pockets of my jacket. Something poked my finger, and I knew exactly what pricked me.

I held the rose Matt had given me the day we'd ridden up to the ridge, the time when his skin grazed mine and I fell into his arms, and we made love. Neither one of us had meant for it to happen, but one thing led to another as we talked about life on that perfect, sunny day. Everything between us felt so right.

The yellow petals that had once been silky were dried, the edges wrinkled and brown but the interior still vibrant and soft. Matt had picked it and tucked it into my hatband.

I put the flower back in my pocket before joining the others. Dad's eyes gleamed in the firelight as he strummed Grandpa's guitar and hummed a cowboy tune.

Grandpa had been burly and a force to be reckoned with, but when he had played his songs, a gentleness drifted into the world through heartfelt lyrics and mellow melodies.

I sat in the Adirondack chair across from my father and put my feet up on the log. "Hi, Dad."

He nodded and kept on singing.

Matt rested his hand on my shoulder. I knew his touch without making eye contact.

"Beautiful night," he said.

Dad fumbled with the cords of a country tune. "I'll get this song right one of these times."

"It's always beautiful here, especially this time of year," I said, quietly. "October will be here before we know it."

Matt's profile softened. "You're right. We're pretty lucky," he said, sitting next to my dad. "There are a lot of people missing out."

"I don't ever want to leave." I gladly wanted to follow in Dad, Grandpa, and Grandma's footsteps.

"Me either," Matt said.

"I was a fool to leave in the first place," Dad said. "Thought I needed something different. Wanted to prove I could live a city life, heal sickness, and make something of myself."

"Maybe you were making sure you weren't missing anything. Besides, if you hadn't strayed, we wouldn't have found Maggie. No regrets there." My thoughts turned inward, but I pushed them away. I tucked my hands in my pockets. "I don't miss Michigan much. And I certainly don't miss the nannies. Do you ever miss being a pediatrician?"

"Sometimes. I liked healing and helping sick children. But I don't miss Michigan much either. This is my home." Dad picked the strings of his guitar and turned the tuning pegs. "And we couldn't keep a nanny long, thanks to your shenanigans."

"I knew it. You *were* a terror." Matt laughed.

"I never said I was an angel, and I do believe I told you about the nannies. They weren't so great." I nuzzled my chin into my fleece. Dad's raised brow made me smile. "What? They weren't." I met the skeptical gazes staring back at me. "Thank goodness Maggie lived next door."

Dad's laughter was met with the howl of a coyote in the distance.

"Let me get this straight. You're taking responsibility for getting your dad and Maggie together?" Matt leaned closer to the fire and warmed his hands.

"Yes. If I hadn't been in her hair all the time,

they might've never gotten together. And besides, I needed her."

"It was a win-win situation," Dad said, shaking his head. "You know what, Matt, she's right. If it weren't for her meddling, things may have turned out differently." Dad's stare brightened.

"Speaking of a win-win situation and meddling, two of the wranglers interested in working with us are also interested in an in-person interview. Our third candidate from Billings took a job with Mr. Amos. He's no longer available."

"So you admit it. You are a pill." Maggie appeared from the shadows, sat next to Dad, and put her feet up on the log; the tips of her cowboy boots jutted to the sky like the mountains at dusk. Her gaze met Matt's stare. "Some angel with a sense of humor must've sent Chloe to keep us all on our toes. Sounds like she hasn't missed a beat."

"I try not to, and I don't think it was an angel. I believe it was a moving van," I said with a chuckle. My heart fluttered at the dimple in Matt's chin when he laughed. Dad put his arm around Maggie, and I held his stare. "We'll figure out a schedule in the morning. You invited your pick. I invited mine, and we'll plan their time here *together*." I rubbed the nip from my hands. "Oh, I almost forgot, they're bringing their own rides."

Dad stood and helped Maggie up. "Sounds like I'm going to need a good night's sleep." He packed up his guitar. "We'll talk about the wranglers tomorrow. As much as I didn't see this coming, it could be interesting. Put on your safety belts, people, my daughter is behind the wheel." Maggie and Dad said goodnight and left the fire, arm in arm.

Matt poked at the dying embers. "Should I put another log on?"

I yawned. "Probably not. I'm pretty tired, too." He reached for me. "What are you doing?"

"Trust me," he said.

I hesitated.

"Come on, now." He lowered his gaze.

"Sorry, but it seems silly. I can get up on my own." One last burst of flames licked the night sky.

"I'm well aware," he whispered.

I laid my hands in his. He wrapped his fingers around mine and tugged. I inched forward in my chair, stood, and tripped into his arms. My hair fell forward and covered my cheeks.

"I like it when you wear a bandana on your head. You sort of look like a pirate."

"Well, I kind of am. I'm scrappy," I said.

"Yet beautiful." Matt caressed my cheek. "I'm

sorry about this afternoon. Guess this baby won't always be bringing out the best in us."

A knot grew at the back of my throat. "You know, pregnancy isn't the kind of surprise every girl hopes for," I said.

"Or guy." He paused. "We did everything we were supposed to do, Chloe. For what it's worth, we have similar bucket lists. Having a baby doesn't mean we have to empty them."

"Wearing another hat will be a lot of work," I said. "Schedules and routines will change. The baby will cry, spit up, and poop, Matt." The fire's final fizzle filled the silence between us. He held my face in his hands.

"Cleaning up after a baby can't be any more daunting than mucking out stalls and chasing strays, except that at some point the baby will be able to talk back." The corner of his mouth lifted. "There'll also be smiles, first words, and laughter. We can make this work. I suggest we take it one day at a time and get some shut-eye. Tomorrow is a new day."

"I don't hate children. I want you to know that," I said.

Matt kissed my forehead, and I made a wish.

"Smooth move with the wranglers, by the way. Who knows, maybe we'll end up with more than one," he said.

I tapped the side of my head. "That's me. I'm always thinking. It'll certainly be interesting."

"By the way, when it's time to wear the parenthood hat, don't take off your ranching hat. Wear 'em both." Matt tugged at the brim of his hat.

"I'll need a hat for being Dad's co-CEO, too. I'll be the queen of multitasking."

We meandered back to the house. The creek's babble took me back to a time when I'd collected rocks from its shallow bed to escape chores and consequences. I knelt, skimmed the water's cool surface with my fingers, plucked a stone from its offerings, and put it in the palm of Matt's hand. "For the sake of practice. I'm giving you part of my load."

"In the business world, we call that delegating."

Matt held my hand. We cradled the smooth stone together. His even temperament was the buoy I clung to when I felt myself treading helplessly. He knew I needed a lifeline tonight, and he'd thrown me one. I'd sleep better for it. Matt's smarts exceeded his master's in business administration. However, the education between us hadn't prepared us for parenthood.

CHAPTER 8

I UNTIED HUCKLEBERRY'S lead, then headed out the door. Matt put his hand on my forearm. I was getting on my horse whether he approved or not. Huckleberry was an old-timer and a gentle one. Matt told Trout he'd catch up later before he untied Trigger, put his left foot in the stirrup, and pulled himself up.

I climbed the mounting block.

"You okay?" Matt nudged Trigger to turn around.

"Yes, why?" I got comfortable in the saddle the color of Huckleberry's freckles.

"Because you never use the block." He rested his hand on his thigh.

"Just tired." I nudged Huckleberry with my heels, and we walked toward the creek. "From what I hear and have read, I can expect to be tired for some time. One more *thing* I need to get used to." I flashed him a forced toothy smile.

Trigger's lazy gait echoed. I looked over at Matt again. He rode high and tight in the saddle.

"I bet if I tried to ditch you, you'd follow me anyway."

"Yup," he replied, playing with the reins. "Where you headed?"

"Thought I'd take a lazy ride along the river." I tugged at the front of my straw hat.

"I love the river. Sounds like a nice idea."

"Suppose I'd better get used to you following me around even more than you did before."

"Like you'd let me," he said with a laugh.

He was right. I wasn't one for hanging on his shirttail or wanting to know where he was every second of the day.

"I can't figure you out, girl—"

"I'm more than a girl."

"You're telling me. You're not like any other woman I've known."

Huckleberry and I veered onto the worn pathway we'd made next to the river over the years. She jerked her head down and snatched up a mouthful of grass. I took a cleansing breath and rested my gaze on the yellow-speckled landscape ahead while she dawdled.

"Come on, girl," I said.

"It's her world, too."

"Thanks for the reminder." I pulled up on the reins and moved her along. She'd lollygag the whole way if I let her. The river flowed over the rocks, playing its Montana tune, drowning Matt's chatter. Snowy peaks in the far distance tickled the blue sky and reminded me of my true stature in the universe. Pine-covered ridges lingered to the left.

Matt and Trigger strolled through the prickly stalks of thistle topped with purple blooms.

"You ever think about riding naked in the river?"

"Where'd that come from? I'm not stripping down to splash in the water with you," I said.

He laughed. "I'm just thinking about cowboy antics and bunkhouse conversation. Can't imagine riding with no britches. But I'd do it if I had to."

Britches. Matt's old soul was emerging.

He pointed to the weeping willow up ahead. "Wanna stop there?"

"Who said anything about stopping?" Riding off into the horizon at any given moment had always been a dream of mine. I imagined Grandpa, Ida May, and cowboys past welcoming me. But in my dream, I'd be able to come back to the ranch after the visit.

"Fine, we can stop on the way back." He wiped his brow with the bandana from his shirt pocket.

"Who said I was coming back?"

"That'd be just like you to ride off into the sunset." He laughed again.

"Nothing wrong with that, cowboy." I stretched my legs and let my feet dangle from the stirrups. Huckleberry had my best interest at heart, and I trusted her to take care of me. I didn't need a wrangler following me around even if he was handsome and attentive. I could handle myself.

"Guess not, but…"

I bobbed to Huckleberry's swaying gait. "But, what?" I pushed my hat back to catch some sun on my face.

"Thought maybe we'd ride into the sunset together," he said.

I sat up a little straighter. My breath caught in my chest. I did what I knew best. I changed the subject. "Sounds like there's some lively talk in the bunkhouse." I took in the landscape, trying to picture a herd of cowboys riding without clothes. I imagined the sunset Matt mentioned, but I couldn't see it.

"There is."

"What else do you talk about?"

Matt took a canteen from his saddlebag. "I'll tell you when we stop at the willow tree on the way back."

"THIS LAZY RIDE along the river sure did shift gears," Matt said as we descended from the ridge. Trigger maneuvered around the rocks in the trail, and Huckleberry followed.

"I guess I changed my mind about where I was going."

"I think you want to make sure I know you wear the pants in this relationship."

I didn't react to his comment.

Huckleberry followed Trigger through the dense pines.

Matt and Trigger trotted into the clearing at the bottom of the ridge. They watched us finish the descent.

"Good girl." I stroked Huckleberry's neck, shiny with sweaty dew. She picked her path carefully and held me steady. "There. We're down." Matt rolled his eyes at me. "Hey, it's my world, too. I want to get in all the riding I can before the doctor tells me to hang up my spurs." I leaned over to poke his knee.

"You should've been a lawyer," he said. "And by the way, we *all* know you think it's your world. Has your dad mentioned anything about your suggestion of becoming co-CEO?"

"Nope. Do you think he took my proposition seriously?"

"Of course he did. Especially after you announced you'd invited two more potential wranglers to the ranch."

"Just trying to find the right guy." The sun shone down like a shower of light. Sweat dripped down my back, and Huckleberry needed a rest. "Are we still gonna stop at the willow?"

"Heck, yeah." He trotted ahead.

Huckleberry didn't feel the need to match Trigger's pace. She pulled at the reins and dipped her head into the sweet grass. Matt dismounted and tied Trigger to a dead log beneath the feathery branches swaying in the breeze.

When Huckleberry stopped, I stood in the stirrups. Matt held my waist until my toes touched solid ground. "Thanks."

He looped my horse's reins around a low branch.

"You don't have to tell me about the bunkhouse if you don't feel like it," I said.

Matt took off his cowboy hat and wiped his brow with his shirtsleeve.

I retrieved the water and apple I'd packed in the saddlebag. I took a bite, then offered the rest to Matt. He declined, so I fed it to Huckleberry. Sweet juice quenched my parched mouth. "There ya' go, girl." I dug into the saddlebag again for the other apple I packed, thinking I'd need a snack too. "Can Trigger have one?"

Matt nodded.

I took a bite of the second apple, then offered the rest to Trigger. He bit into it, and half of it fell to the ground. He swished his tail and lifted his back left hoof.

Matt took my hand and led me to the riverbank, where we sat side by side beneath the green canopy. "This tree seems bigger every time I stop here," he said. "Makes me feel safe when I'm tucked beneath the shade."

I drank from my canteen. "I know what you mean," I said.

"You shouldn't be so stubborn." He leaned back against the tree trunk. "You can't force what was meant or not meant to be."

"I can't help it," I said. "I've always been this way. You, of all people, should know that."

"No wonder you couldn't keep a nanny."

"Touché." I pulled my legs to my chest, then rested my chin on my knees. Water pushed over the river rocks like I rolled over whatever stood in my way. Matt took off his hat and put it on the ground next to him. He fingered the braided leather band.

"Can you imagine living in a different century

and moving cattle? Think about it. The conditions, the drives, the pay, what those wranglers did to earn a living and survive. Makes my blood flow." Matt's eyes glimmered. "Boy, would I have liked to witness an 1800s cattle drive or two up close and in person."

"Maybe you did. I could picture you living back then," I said.

"I didn't know you believed in stuff like that." Matt plucked a long strand of grass from the ground.

"You'd be surprised. You should be inside my head."

"Not sure that's someplace I need to be." He tucked the blade of grass in his hatband. "Your words tell me one thing, Chloe McIntyre, but your eyes say something else." Matt picked a gangly golden wildflower and tucked it into the leather band on my hat. The buttery petals resembled bursts of light shooting from the sun. "Something to remember the day by," he said.

"The last time you gave me a flower, I got pregnant."

"This one will remind you that simple things can help us get through tough times."

He mentioned the word *us* again. The connotation made my heart skip a beat. "You're sweet," I said.

"Maybe, but remember, I'm also the guy who'd strip off his clothes with the other cowboys and ride wild through the cold Montana rivers."

"You let me know how that goes, cowboy."

He touched my cheek. The breeze picked up, and goose bumps covered the nape of my neck. Matt's boyish gaze alluded to a bounty of secrets he savored. He put his arm around me, and I leaned into him.

"I'm this ranch and this ranch is me," I said, swallowing away the building tension. "I watched every move my grandpa made. I watched my dad learn from his father, too."

"I know."

Matt pulled me closer, and I rested my head against his. His humming lulled me. The scent of sage drifted past, and the weight lifted from my shoulders.

"If I fall asleep, don't wake me. Everything is perfect in this moment." The breeze caressed my cheek like Grandpa's touch before he'd tuck me in on a starry night. The scent of leather and after-shave tickled my senses. My mind wandered.

"I know, Grandpa. I will," I whispered.

"Chloe."

I pretended not to hear Matt. *Stay a little longer, Grandpa.* His dreamy presence delivered a familiar kiss to my cheek, his soft whiskers brushed against my skin. Grandma stood in the background. Heaven tugged at the corner of my mouth. I pressed my eyes tighter as a shadow whisked them away.

Don't go.

"Chloe," Matt said again.

I opened my eyes to let the world in. Reality stung like lemon juice on the tiniest of cuts, and I pushed it away along with a strand of hair from my cheek.

"Hey, you okay? You're mumbling about something."

I scanned the horizon. "It wasn't *just* something. They were here."

"Who was here?"

"You wouldn't believe me if I told you." I searched the clouds rolling west in the sky.

"Try me," Matt said, squeezing my shoulder.

I nuzzled into his neck. "Nope, it wasn't you. No musk there."

"What?" His brow creased.

"Just checking," I said. "I smelled my grandpa's aftershave, and Ida May was with him."

Huckleberry whinnied then pawed at the ground. I had a feeling I wasn't alone when it came to sensing my grandparents.

"We should get back. Somebody might be wondering where we are," I said.

"You're probably right." Matt put on his hat, then stood.

He offered me a hand, and I took it. "Matt," I said, taking a step closer to him. Standing nose to nose and eye to eye, I had to say it one more time. "They were both here."

"When you want something badly enough and you wish upon a starry sky night after night, you're bound to have at least one wish come true."

"I don't think wishing on the stars has anything to do with it." I untied the horses.

"I believe you." Matt adjusted Trigger's girth.

"I hope they come back."

"They will. Good ole Winston wouldn't leave your side for a whole herd of cattle. And from the stories I've heard, Ida May was just as protective when it came to watching over your daddy."

"Thank you," I said, touching his chin. Matt took my hand, pressed it to his lips. He was starting to feel like more than my child's father.

"You're welcome. Now let's get you back on that horse." He cupped his hands. "Come on, darlin'. Show me what you got."

I grabbed the horn and hoisted myself up. "I know you think I shouldn't be riding. I've read articles, and Dr. Hennessey said she's had other patients who've ridden. Their babies have been fine, healthy as can be." The saddle creaked as I settled in. "She'll confirm it when we see her. Maybe that will ease your mind." I set my feet in the stirrups.

Matt stayed quiet.

"Aren't you going to say anything?"

He rested his hand on my thigh. "I believe you. I've done my own research. And thanks for using the mounting block back there. I know you didn't need it. I appreciate the effort when it comes to being careful."

"I forgot, you're the smart one in the bunch with that business degree." I flipped his cowboy hat from his brow.

"A piece of paper stamped by a university doesn't necessarily make me brainier than the next guy—or you," he said. "But no crazy stuff and no riding alone. I mean it."

"I'd like to think my degree counts for something. I worked my buns off. Paying attention in school was demanding," I answered.

Matt mounted Trigger and nudged him to walk by my side.

"You know not riding crazy and not riding alone are pretty much everyday rules around here," I added.

"I know, and you've broken those rules plenty."

We said little on the way home, although I lifted my chin often. Matt just might be the best man I'd ever met besides Dad and Grandpa.

CHAPTER 9

T HE SUNRISE MELTED away the early morning fog. I planted my foot on the bottom rail of the fence and leaned against it. I rested my chin on my hands and waited for Dad, Trout, Matt, Tristan, Quinn, and Justin. We had planned on moving the cattle to the north pasture, and they were late. Maggie was staying behind to garden and work on her coffee table book depicting the Montana landscape with the photos she'd been taking since she moved here. She said pulling weeds was like editing, and cutting and arranging flowers helped her organize her thoughts.

I checked my watch, attached the radio to my belt, mounted Gypsy, and rode out without them. They'd know where to find me.

I'd managed to run the horses with a queasy stomach earlier, and the slow ride alone lifted my mood. Solo time with my best girl was better than any medicine. I braided strands of her mane until the sound of hooves were upon us. Justin rode up alongside me.

"So now you're gonna wrangle solo?"

"Y'all were dillydallying," I answered.

Justin leaned forward on the horn of his saddle and pushed his cowboy hat back. "Admit it, you prefer being a lone ranger. No one to check up on you. No one to answer to. This ranch ain't nothing but one big henhouse, and henhouses have occasional visitors. But your secret is safe with me. I saw you ride your horse up the mountain this morning and get sick."

I took in Justin's boyish grin that hadn't changed since the day I'd met him. I let out a grunt I didn't know I was capable of. "Who else knows?"

"Not sure, but I'm not one to cluck." He pushed his hat back. "Morning sickness or no morning sickness, you're a heck of a lot prettier than my brother or Trout. Doubt the two new guys you invited will be better-looking than you, either."

"You're such a charmer." I fiddled with the reins.

"Why, thank you, ma'am." He tugged his hat down. "Looks like your daddy and his posse aren't far behind. If you need me to cover, I've got your back."

"Thanks. You're a good friend."

Justin and I waited for Dad, Trout, Matt, Tristan, and Quinn to catch up. We rode together and discussed the hiccups we might face moving the cattle. Gypsy and I were sandwiched between the six men. To my right, Justin, Matt, and Quinn were eager to move the cattle efficiently, making room in the day for loose ends. To my left, Dad and Trout listened to Tristan's strategy for an effective transition to minimize the strays. I didn't join in with their agreeable remarks.

Matt nudged Trigger with his heels, then took off in a full canter to the head of the herd. The thunder of Trigger's gallop beat upon the earth like a war drum. Justin, Trout, and Quinn followed.

I eyed Tristan. I had plenty of strategy up my sleeve, too. "We could always use a feed truck. Haven't met an animal who doesn't like food."

"Although an interesting concept"—Tristan pushed his hat back from his forehead—"I believe feeding 'em to move along will backfire in the future. They'll expect it, and when it's not there, what's the motivation?"

"I'm not saying bring out a feed truck every time. Just when we know the transition can be dicey depending on the weather or pace. Mix it up. Give 'em something they don't get every day." My gaze met Dad's.

"Something to think about." Dad scratched his chin and straightened his posture.

My dad's reaction meant he took my suggestion seriously. I patted Gypsy's neck and settled into my basket-woven, tooled saddle Grandpa had given me for my twenty-first birthday, my boots snugly tucked into the heavy, rawhide stirrups. Gypsy whinnied; she was ready to work, and so was I. Swaying to Gypsy's easy stride was like listening to a favorite tune, and I couldn't wait for the dancing to begin.

Tristan clicked his tongue at Hitch, and they rode round the rear of the herd.

Dad circled to ride alongside me.

"I like your suggestion. Just wondering if we'd need special equipment."

"Dad, we've cut our trails and pathways. Using the wagon is an option. We have the horsepower. If we need a truck, we've got the funds."

Dad tipped his hat. "Let's chat later. The rest of the crew is gonna think you're getting special treatment if I let you ladies dillydally."

"Wouldn't want that," I said. "You'll know where to find me if you need me." I checked to make sure the radio was still clipped to my belt. "Let's step it up, sister." With a click of my teeth, Gypsy eased into a pleasing trot.

The breeze against my cheeks breathed new life. I wrapped my right hand in Gypsy's mane, whipped the tails of the reins against her side, then held on. Gypsy and I found our rhythm and rode past moseying white horns and grazing rawhide, their presence mystical, like ghostly ancestors from a long-ago era nestled in the quilted lush hills of Ireland.

I rode like fury over to the cattle bringing up the rear, where Gypsy and I kept our distance. Matt circled back and positioned himself between me and the herd. His intent to prevent my intervention was clear. I nudged Gypsy and clicked my tongue to maintain our loping strides.

"Ya," Matt's voice boomed. Trigger's ears perked up.

Gypsy followed suit. I held steady. "Come on, girl," I muttered even though no one could hear me over the lowing cattle.

Gypsy pulled ahead, and I rode far in front of the herd, as if there were a finish line. Gypsy slowed to a trot in the open meadow and then a content strut. She'd enjoyed the run, too.

"Hey," Tristan shouted, "what was that?"

He sauntered up next to us. Hitch was about two hands taller than my Gypsy. The gleam in his eye and the tilt of his head read arrogance, but neither Gypsy nor I were intimidated.

"Riding." The hair stood up on my forearms.

"Not sure this is the place for a woman," he said, staring straight ahead.

"I'm sure it is." I matched his intensity and gestured for Trout.

Tristan didn't answer.

"You sure you're Justin's brother?"

"Yep," he answered.

"FYI, I'm not here on a trial basis," I informed him. "Your wrangling technique isn't mine. And I'm sure the wranglers joining us tomorrow will have their own ideas about how to get things done." Holding my tongue never came easy. "Sometimes the bottom line is just getting the job done."

"Are you always this pleasant?"

"Pretty much." I was sure Dad would hear about this.

"Seriously, what are you doing out here? Wouldn't you rather be back home baking or gardening?" he asked with a glint in his eye.

"Nope. This is my country. When I bake, there tends to be smoke. And I don't have a green thumb." I fixated on the mountains and gave Trout the high sign to join me.

"Hey, kid," Trout called. "Everything looks

grand from this view. Can't imagine you need anything from me." His horse, Tupelo Honey, snorted as if she were disgusted with the interruption.

"You're right. I got this covered," I said.

Trout rode away, and I turned my attention back to Tristan. I inspected every inch of him, the scar on the back of his left hand, the flex in his jaw when chugging water from a canteen, the muddy heels of his boots. He was going to be a challenge, and I would give him a run for his money. If he voiced an idea to improve the ranch, I'd voice two. I'd show my dad the savvy and brawn a co-CEO needed. I sat a little taller and nodded to Matt as he rode past.

"Are you two together?" Tristan asked.

"What does that have to do with wrangling?"

"Nothing." He sighed. "I just wanted a bigger picture. Didn't mean to be personal."

"Working for my daddy means working for me, too," I said.

"You're not the only one who likes a challenge. Can't wait to meet my competition." He and Hitch trotted ahead.

Matt had reached the stream's edge, dismounted, taken off his hat, and wiped his forehead. Gypsy and I meandered his way. I stood in my stirrups, trying to air out my backside.

Matt grabbed Gypsy's bridle. "What are you doing, Chloe?" He gritted his teeth. "When are you going to realize this isn't all about you? There's nothing to prove here."

I swung my right foot over the saddle. Matt's hands were on my waist. "I can get down," I said.

"I know. I'm just trying to—"

"I know what you're doing. I guess we should've defined *crazy* riding. I didn't do anything out of the normal." Matt meant well. I got that. I understood my boundaries even if he didn't. We'd eventually agree on a common ground. "I love doing my job. And after you rode off, I had a great idea about moving the cattle."

Matt took the reins from me, then led the horses to water. I followed. Wispy grass brushed against my shins. My jeans stuck to my sweaty skin. I sat on the dead log and stretched my legs. He was right in some ways. "You're just being protective. I get it."

"For as long as I've known you, you're happier with the wind in your hair and no one in tow. You thrive on being you. Independence should be your middle name."

"You act like there's something wrong with that," I said.

Matt wrapped the reins around a limb near the water. Gypsy stepped into the stream, her chocolate brown eyes an all-knowing haven. Matt sat, rested his elbows on his knees, and hung his head.

"Fine, whatever. Your head is so thick, nothing I'm gonna say will matter," he said.

Matt's words cut me. "I'm sorry. I was doing fine, moseying along, and then you were there between the herd and me. Nothing happened."

"Whatever," he mumbled.

"It's not *whatever*. I feel like you're watching everything I do," I said. "I have to be me. I can't change being pregnant and doing my job."

"But you can change how you treat this pregnancy and modify your job while you're expecting. No one will think any less of you. Chloe, you have all the time in the world to be you. Can't you just push pause for the time being?"

"No, *I* can't." The articles I'd read about women who rode while pregnant—I would be one of them. I'd write the article if someone asked me to. "Soon, there'll be a list of things I won't be able to do or shouldn't do. That's when I'll curb my lifestyle."

Matt took off his hat and ran his fingers through his thick hair.

I picked up a rock and tossed it in the water.

"I don't want you to lose the baby," he whispered.

"What?"

"I don't want you to lose the baby," he said louder.

I bit the inside of my cheek. Did he love me, too? If he did, why didn't he tell me? But I wasn't ready for those words either. I had to understand this layer of our relationship before hopping ahead to the next chapter, and the chapters were already out of order.

"I never thought in a million years you'd get pregnant. I'm sorry."

"It's not your fault," I said. "We're in this together."

"I know. I'm sorry because I know how you feel about having children."

"Yeah, well, we don't always get what we want," I said. "My dad can tell us some stories to prove it. We all have stories." The corner of my lip curled, and my gaze met his. "Not funny. Okay then." I shrugged. "Me not wanting kids doesn't matter now."

Matt's left dimple appeared. "Really?"

I nodded. "Really."

"Do you think your dad will fire me?"

I hadn't thought of Matt losing his job. "That's

what you're worried about? He would never."

"Well, he can't fire you. You're his daughter."

"If it makes you feel better, yes, he could. Kick me out. Disown me. Not talk to me anymore. Am I making you feel any better?" My shoulders fell forward.

Matt put his hat back on. "The other day you suggested I should try being inside your head." He paused. "Do you remember?"

"Sure do, and I can't say I blame you for declining the invite."

"What do you say we try getting inside each other's heads a little more often? Maybe we'd understand some things we haven't considered."

"Sure," I said. "This baby adventure sure is complicated." I stood. "Before I digest anything more, I should get on my horse. Best therapy ever." I held out my hand to Matt and helped him up. "Let's go, cowboy."

"When we head back, will you please take it easy?"

"You worry too much," I said, stretching my back.

"Maybe I do"—he lowered his gaze—"but humor me."

"Fine. I'll see what I can do."

"You are such a pain, Chloe McIntyre."

"I know. And FYI, Tristan and I didn't get off to the best start today."

"I wouldn't expect anything less. Sounds like we got ourselves a top-notch wrangler on board."

"We'll find out. The other two candidates are arriving tonight, and I'm looking forward to seeing them in action," I said.

CHAPTER 10

D AD AND I discussed using a feed truck to move the cattle while working. I'd contacted Mosley, a rancher we collaborated with from time to time, for input regarding the idea. He'd helped us in the past, and Dad trusted him. With the information, we could construct a timeline for implementation. Confident that Dad would be receptive, I strutted to the house and into Dad's office after feeding the horses.

"Hey, Dad. Hi, Maggie. We did well today. The cattle were cooperative. I have some specifics on the feed truck."

"We've got other pressing matters." His left eyebrow shot up.

"Is Glad okay?" I asked.

Gladiola lived in Michigan. Maggie worried about her mother's health since Glad's trips to the ranch slowed. So did I. She claimed her social life took over her calendar, but Maggie kept after her to visit.

"My mom is fine." Maggie lowered herself into

the leather chair next to the desk and nibbled on her thumbnail. I sat in Grandpa's rocking chair, where he'd told me stories of Montana, Ida May, and how he'd built the ranch and raised my dad.

Dad massaged his temples. His jaw flexed as the vein in his neck bulged. And I waited. The knot in my belly tightened.

Dad looked over to Maggie, who lowered her gaze and rubbed her nape. "I can't believe you didn't tell me," he said.

"Kind of not my deal," she said.

"You could've given me a hint, but no, I had to find out from Tristan." Dad leaned against his desk. "When were you going to tell me you're pregnant, Chloe?" He pushed papers around as if he'd misplaced a recent invoice.

"I tried to tell you the other day in the barn, but we got interrupted. I'm sorry." Knowing that was a mere excuse, I pushed my shoulders against the back of the chair. "How did Tristan know?"

Dad paced.

"I'm not trying to change the subject. I want to know. This is none of his business," I said. A flash of heat singed my cheeks.

"Does it matter?" Dad rubbed his whiskery chin. "It doesn't change the situation."

"It may not change the situation, but I'd like to know."

"He overheard you and Matt talking in the barn. He thought I knew," Dad explained. "He only mentioned it because he thought you'd suggested a feed truck to cut back on riding. He thought it was your way of being in the pasture and not on the back of a horse." Dad tucked his hands in his back pockets.

Maggie's stare offered silent support to both Dad and me.

"Being pregnant and lightening my load wasn't why I mentioned a feed truck." I held his stare. "This baby wasn't planned. Accidents happen even if you do—" I pinched the bridge of my nose, then hurried to finish my sentence. "Take precautions." My chest ached; I'd let my father down. I was certain my surprise pregnancy was triggering memories from his rocky past with my mother. "So now what? Am I banished from the house? Are you going to stop talking to me?"

Dad grimaced. "You're not banished."

"I'm ready for the lecture. You might as well let me have it," I said.

"I don't think you need a lecture." His tone softened. "Sounds like you've already taken care of that from your end." He leaned against his desk. "Have you and Matt talked about getting married?"

"I don't want to get married." I covered my face, and my hair fell forward. My dad had married my mother when they found out she was expecting me. After taking a deep breath, I looked at him. "I'm sorry, Dad. The last thing I want is a marriage proposal from Matt because he thinks he has to marry me."

A dark shadow passed over Dad's face.

"I know you don't want to hear that I'm pregnant and there's no husband. I'm sorry. My head's not in the place where two people might choose to get married. Neither is Matt's. Jumping from the fire to the frying pan isn't going to magically construct the foundation needed to raise a child."

Dad fidgeted with the horseshoe paperweight holding down unopened mail and avoided eye contact.

"Chloe—" He hesitated.

"Go ahead say it."

"You're right. I didn't want to hear that you're pregnant. Not because there'll be a child to raise, but because I know this isn't what you wanted. When you're disappointed, I am, too. When you hurt, I hurt. When you're conflicted, I'm frustrated. But you'll understand shortly, and you'll spend your life feeling for your own child."

I bit my lip and fixated on the knot in the wood

of Dad's desk. Nothing made sense. This baby perpetuated a seemingly never-ending roller coaster of emotion. Now, I didn't know what I felt. The one thing I knew for certain was I'd outgrow my pants sooner than later and I detested shopping.

Dad took my hands in his, and I stood. He wrapped his arms around me, whispered my name, and stroked my hair. "You are my daughter with a love for animals, the open range, and her family."

The phone rang, and Maggie answered it. She spoke softly as Dad's familiar words echoed in my head: *everything happens for a reason.*

"I'm sorry I didn't come to you sooner," I said.

"Me too."

Maggie ended the call, her mouth lined with worry.

"Is something wrong?" I asked.

Maggie leaned on the desk. A thin smile crept into the seam of her lips. "I can't believe it. I've been after that woman to get out here for some time now, and she's going to do it." Her eyes flickered with anticipation. "When it rains it pours."

Dad put his arm around my shoulder and pulled me close.

"Give it to me straight," he said.

"Mom is coming to visit," Maggie said.

"Good for her." Dad's approval eased the tension between us. "We could use some more excitement around here. How do you think she'd feel about manning a feed truck?" He walked across the room to the minibar nestled in the shelves lined with books and family photos. "It's five o'clock somewhere, and we should celebrate Glad's travel plans. Chloe, we'll discuss the feed truck later. It's got promise."

"Glad is coming?" I asked.

Maggie nodded. "She's got a first-class plane ticket and can't wait to get out here."

Dad raised his cocktail. "Here's to another able body on the ranch."

Maggie giggled and took my hands in hers. "I told you before, your dad and I will be here for you."

"I know, but it's a strange feeling knowing I'm going to have a baby." I looked at my dad. There wasn't anything there that appeared to judge me. I was sure he had worries and advice, and I was sure he would air his thoughts later. "Dad, would it be okay if I excused myself?"

"There's something I'd like you to do before you call it a day." He took a hard swallow of bourbon.

"What?"

"Our friends Butch and Sundance have found themselves another patch of burrs," he said.

"Someone else has got to learn how to handle those two," I moaned.

Dad smirked. "You're the only one they'll let touch their tails. The honor is all yours, sweetheart."

"Will it get me the title of co-CEO?"

Dad's brow dipped.

Trout knocked on the doorframe. "You ready for an evening smoke, son?"

The longing in Dad's gaze tugged at my heart as Trout handed him one of the cigars tucked in his shirt pocket. It was as if Grandpa were standing alongside them, present in the conversation.

"Okay then, you're not ready. I'll go take care of the delinquents." I left the office and pulled my bandana from my back pocket. The weight on my shoulders seemed lighter. Maybe Tristan had done me a favor. I tucked my hair behind my ears and tied the black-and-white paisley cloth around my head, then pushed it up on my forehead until it was in the right spot. "Dad and Maggie aren't the only ones growing older." I inspected my face in the foyer mirror. This was one of those times I realized I had to make room for the future even if I wanted to hang on to the past.

Maggie's laugh echoed through the hallway. The aroma of woody cigars blossomed in the air. I patted my belly and whispered to myself, "It is what it is. We're in this together, kid."

Dad tapped me on the shoulder. "I'd like to discuss one more thing with you."

I turned on a heel to see him better. "What's up?"

"About the co-CEO position you suggested."

Before I could say anything, he touched my lips with his finger.

"Here me out before you say anything. I'm not getting any younger, and your granddad would want me to be proactive regarding the ranch. This baby will change a lot around here. Raising children and working full-time is a tall order."

"You worked full-time and raised me."

"Exactly. And you missed out on some things I wouldn't want your children to miss out on. They'll need their momma."

"Wait a minute. Who said anything about *children*? Now you've got me raising more than one?"

"That's not what I meant. What I meant to say was, this baby will need its momma, and this ranch isn't going anywhere while you're around. I've asked Matt to consider taking the position as co-CEO."

"Seriously?"

"Matt's got a fine head on his shoulders, and with a baby on the way, he's going to want to stick around. Having you both on board makes sense." He paused. "Before you say anything, making him co-CEO doesn't make you any less important. It ensures you'll have another competent wrangler invested in what means most to you when the time comes."

Matt had just secured everything I had ever wanted.

CHAPTER 11

ABOUT AN HOUR after I started working on Sundance's tail, Tristan waltzed into the barn. I kept my head down despite the crick in my neck. The daunting task of de-burring matted tails exceeded my patience. Dad's news about asking Matt to be co-CEO was fresh and stung.

"I'm sorry if I said something I wasn't supposed to." Tristan's boot heels clicked against the dusty floor.

Sundance shifted her weight. I moved aside, staying clear of her hind legs. I picked strands from another prickly bulb lodged in her wavy hair and tossed it into the bucket.

My fingers worked quickly and carefully. Sundance's patience ran hot and cold, even with me.

"Is there something else you wanted to talk to me about? I'd like to finish this up," I said.

"I thought your dad knew."

I clipped the last burr from her tail. My gaze met his. "He didn't." I brushed out Sundance's tail, then trimmed it.

"Matt's a lucky guy," he said.

I didn't acknowledge him. I put my arm under Sundance's tail, wanting to clip it a bit shorter than usual, and measured out the final cut.

"Seriously, you're quite the catch."

I trimmed the last bit of uneven hair, then patted her rump. "You don't know anything about me."

"Look, I'm doing my best here to apologize." He tucked his gloves in his back pocket. "Seriously, someday this ranch will all be yours."

I scowled. "You should've stopped at the apology." I latched the door to Sundance's stall and started deburring Butch. "You're such an instigator," I said.

"You must be talking to the horse." Tristan planted his hands on his hips.

I shrugged, worked a ball of prickly bulbs free from Butch's tail, and dropped them in the bucket. He craned his neck to see me better and gave a little kick in Tristan's direction. I couldn't help but grin.

"In case you're wondering, I haven't changed my mind about taking the position here. I'm exactly what this place needs, and I'd be honored to work with my little brother even though he's not so little anymore. Working alongside fellow wranglers gunning for the job doesn't bother me."

"You sure you don't mind working with or for a woman?" I picked at the next snag of burrs. "You need to watch where you're walking."

"Justin didn't mention you don't have a filter. Just trying to be straight with you, ma'am." He tipped his hat and turned to walk away.

"What's going on in here?" Matt poked his head in the barn door.

I wondered how much he had heard.

"Ask her," Tristan said, jabbing his thumb in my direction. "You sure do have your hands full." He left the barn and didn't look back.

"Not sure how he can be related to Justin." My enunciation was loud and clear.

"He did apologize. I'm not sure he could do much more," Matt said.

I patted Butch's rump. "Stand still." I used the razor to free the last few prickly bulbs, brushed out his tail, and trimmed the end. "We're going shorter than usual with you, too," I told the horse. "Maybe you'll be less likely to find the burrs."

"Looks like a professional's work," Matt said.

"That's me. Professional." I handed him the lead, and we walked Butch out to the corral, where he pressed his chin to my hip. "Yes, you can have some sugar." I kissed my hand and touched his muzzle. Matt laughed. Butch watched my hand disappear into my pocket. After his treat, he ran off.

Matt's boots kicked up dust as he scuffled along. No doubt, he was tired from working extra hours, filling in, thinking about becoming a daddy, and now he had Dad's offer floating around inside his handsome head.

"You know, Tristan's just trying to fit in," he finally said.

I wrinkled my nose at him.

"He's new. He wants you to think he's a hotshot, knows a lot, which he does. You should listen to him."

I stopped in my tracks. "What?"

"Stop looking at me like that. I just mean *listen*. Not in the sense that you have to do what he says, but hear him out. He's got some good ideas." Matt rubbed his chin. "He's trying to make a good impression."

I grimaced. "Well, that's some impression."

"You're not out there with us all the time or in the bunkhouse. You don't hear the guys talking." Matt stopped and turned. The sunlight softened his face. His chiseled jaw relaxed. "At least the news is out there now. Not gonna lie, it's been a little awkward with your dad. I wasn't quite sure what to say to him during our chat. I think it went pretty good."

"I'd say it went really well for you. Co-CEO. That's an honor. Are you going to accept Dad's offer?" I sat down on the tack box. The soles of my boots scraped against the floor.

"I don't know. I don't think I have to decide today. Besides, isn't that something we should talk about?"

"Yes. And thank you." I relaxed my shoulders and took a deep breath. "Does everyone know about the baby? Who am I kidding? Of course, everyone knows. It is what it is." I saw hurt in his eyes and realized how I must've sounded. "I'm sorry," I said.

Matt sat next to me and held my hand. "I'm not scared to be someone's father. No, we didn't plan this. Yes, we thought we were covered, but for whatever the reason, there's a baby. You're not in this alone. You'll be a great mom."

He kissed my forehead, and I laid my head on his shoulder. "Thank you."

"Now that's more like it. A little sugar goes a long way," he said.

"Don't I know it," I mumbled.

Sundance poked her head out of the stall. I gave her some sugar. "You're staying in there until

Butch is done being irritated with me. You're such a follower."

"You've got them all figured out."

"I wish." I sat up and pushed my shoulders back. "Am I a leader or follower?"

"Truth? Leader and instigator."

"Hey, I don't believe instigator was a choice."

"It wasn't, but it's true. And I have a sneaking suspicion you and Tristan are more alike than you think."

"Two jabs in one blow. I'd better duck and weave before the next one comes my way." I got up to organize the tack. "Glad's coming to visit. I can't wait for her to get here."

"You know, Butch and Sundance probably find mischief on purpose and balk at the rest of us because they know you'll be around to fix them up, and then reward them."

Matt patted my bottom. Warmth from his touch penetrated my jeans.

"You better be careful. We don't need any more trouble." I skipped away.

"Honey, we're already knee-deep," Matt said.

Dad walked into the barn. "Knee-deep in what?"

"You know, *stuff*," I answered. My cheeks warmed as he lifted his brow.

"Now is as good a time as any since you're both together," Dad said.

Matt tossed a bale of hay into the empty stall, then stood beside me.

"I want you two to know—" Dad tucked his fingers into his front pockets after a long pause. "Even though your situation isn't ideal, you're both adults. I have my own ideas, but I'll do my best to stay out of it. But I'm here if you need me." He kicked at the floorboard, then looked at Matt sternly.

Matt reciprocated Dad's serious stare. Dad patted him on the back and called him *son*. Matt nodded and shook Dad's hand.

"Seems you two had quite the conversation without me," I said. They both stared at me, the glint in their eyes all-telling.

"Yeah," they answered simultaneously.

Dad and Matt's alliance was stronger than ever. "That's a little scary." Coal purred and walked between my legs. I picked her up and held her nose to mine. She mewed. "We could match their wit any day," I told her.

"I don't doubt that," Dad said. "It's nice to see you acting a little more like your old self."

Matt nudged me, and I smiled.

"Butch and Sundance are done. Coal, you're in

charge of those two. Keep them out of the burrs." Coal jumped from my arms.

"You two need a chore?" Dad asked.

"Sure, what do you have in mind?" Matt scratched his chin.

"Could you take the truck and ride out to check the ditches that keep giving us trouble? The last thing we need is a herd on the loose."

"Already on my list," Matt answered. "Chloe, you wanna go?"

"Can I hit the can first?" I asked.

Dad winced. "She's been hanging around too many men."

Matt laughed. "I'll be in the truck."

I scooted out the door and across the path back to the house. Tristan was in the front pasture, riding bareback, working with Casanova. He wasn't like any other cowboy on the 617 Ranch. He took advantage of every nook and cranny in the day. Taking a break meant tackling his personal agenda.

Inside, Maggie rummaged through the refrigerator. "Hey, what are you up to?"

"Matt and I are going to check the ditches for Dad."

"What's with the long face?"

I leaned against the counter. "Dad asked Matt

to be his co-CEO. Nothing is going as planned. Where does that leave me?”

Maggie peeled carrots. Thin orange ribbons filled her bowl of scraps for the compost. “Your dad’s got your best interest at heart. You don’t need a title, Chloe.”

“I think I do.”

CHAPTER 12

OUR GUEST WRANGLERS, Levi Chisum and Silas McNeilly, arrived last night after dinner to get a lay of the land. They had toured the property with Matt, bunked with the guys, and I was hoping to get an earful this morning.

I stood with Gypsy in the downy blanket of fog shrouding the sleepy landscape. Swaddled in a serene stillness where everyday concerns didn't exist, this 'tween time was my favorite time of day. Tristan rode up on Hitch. He donned a long trench and spurs. He'd dressed might properly for the interview.

He tugged at the brim of his hat. "Good morning."

"Hey there. Where you been hiding the fancy chaps?"

"Thought I should put my best foot forward. I hear the gal who runs this place with her daddy is a tough nut."

"You ain't kidding," Trout said, slinging Daddy's saddle on Breeze.

"I'm not one to be impressed by expensive leather or fancy clothes. It's who's perched *in* the saddle and their skills that count."

Silas appeared from the haze like an unsung hero. With a dip of his head, he slapped his gloves across his thigh. "Morning."

"You ready for the day, cowboy?" I reached out to shake his hand. His thick grip was that of a man who was sure of himself. He was almost a head taller and burlier than any wrangler I'd met. His straw cowboy hat hid a full head of red hair, but not his manicured beard.

"Cisco is saddled and ready to go. The troughs have fresh water. Figured I'd make myself useful while waiting for the others."

"Great. They'll appreciate your efforts. When we go out this morning, I'd like you to stick with me. We'll ride up the mountain and round up the strays at the top. Levi will stay close to my dad. Where is Levi?" My gaze met Tristan's.

Silas pushed his hat back and scratched his forehead. "Um, he was getting duded up when I left the bunkhouse. If fashion's gonna win me the job, thanks for the opportunity. I would've liked it here."

Silas's worn denim pleased me fine. "Fashion won't win you anything here." My gaze met

Tristan's, again.

"Good morning." Dad walked toward us. Samson waddled at his side with his nose in the air, catching the morning sniffs. Dad shook Silas's hand. "Hope you slept okay."

"Slept great. That's a nice bunkhouse compared to some of the places I've been."

"Where've you been?" I patted Gypsy's hind end.

"I've been on drives where I stayed in rustic cabins to fancy shanties with running water. Nothing like a cold shower to wash off the day. I figure if I have a place to lay my head, it's a good day. Excuse me." Silas glanced over his shoulder. He made smooching sounds before releasing a sharp whistle. Cisco stepped from the foggy mist with a bowed head.

"He certainly knows how to make an entrance." I rested my hands on my hips. "Very Hollywood."

"Ain't nothing Hollywood about us. No, ma'am. Just a cowboy and his trusted companion working the land for honest wages where we're needed," Silas replied.

I smiled at my dad.

Levi sauntered out of the barn with his gray dapple, Tattoo. I'd spoken too soon. These two definitely oozed Hollywood glam. Levi's shiny spurs jangled with each step, his gleaming white teeth a beacon for those lost in a storm. Dad greeted him. Samson sat at Levi's feet and drooled. This was a photo opportunity, and Maggie was missing it.

"Morning, Levi. Welcome." I shook his hand. His blue gaze was eagerly nervous. His cologne wafted around me like a department store counter at a pricy mall.

"Thanks for having me. Can't wait to get working," he said.

Trout stood to the side and sized up the men in his own way.

"Where's Matt?" I asked.

"He's already at the base of the mountain," Tristan answered. "Said he'd meet us there." Tristan set his reins and circled. "Shall we? I know this is your favorite part of the day."

"You're gonna have to do more than butter me up." I mounted Gypsy. "Follow me. Silas and I will comb the slope. Levi, you stay with my dad. The horses are pretty good about not running off, but if we need to round any of them up, follow Tristan's lead."

"Guess you do like a little buttering up," Tristan said.

"Just assessing your skills." I hooked the radio to the back of my belt.

"I'll man the gate," Trout said.

"You're a good man and the perfect gatekeeper." Dad tipped his hat to our beloved foreman.

"Thanks, son." Trout's moustache twitched. "Just an old-timer willing to let the youngsters take the brunt."

Silas and I took the lead. Matt's silhouette appeared in the foggy mist drifting toward the sunrise. Tristan rode alone not too far away. I contemplated his distant demeanor as he homed in on the job ahead.

"You want me to do anything else besides *take the lead*?" Tristan asked.

"Nope. Just be yourself," I answered.

"I'll try to be on my best behavior." He flashed a wry smile and rode ahead.

"He seems pretty comfortable," Silas said.

"So it would appear." I fingered Gypsy's mane. "Have you ever worked with a difficult person?"

Silas nodded. "Sure have. Sometimes the cattle are easier to wrangle than the guys who are supposed to have your back."

"So when you're working with a difficult person, how do you handle them?"

Silas tugged at the brim of his hat. "With all

due respect, Ms. McIntyre, my job is cattle, not wrangling cattlemen. I can hold my own, and I'm not shy about speaking up, but I've never felt it was my place to handle another hired hand."

I pointed to the sandy rut ahead. "Follow me up the trail. My Huckleberry should be straggling near the ridge up ahead. She'd rather stay out here all day and wander than be a follower." The shaggy evergreen branches tickled my cheek, and the sweet scent of sage washed over me. "Can't say I blame her." Gypsy maneuvered over the gnarly tree roots and rocks. "Your application named seven ranches you worked. Which one did you like best and why?"

"Ten Gallon, I suppose. Three hundred head of cattle and never a dull moment."

"Why'd you leave?"

"It was time to move on. Never stayed in one place too long." Silas patted his horse's shoulder.

"How long is too long? Working with us would be a long-term commitment."

"I was there three years."

I pulled back on Gypsy. "Why was it time to move on? Humor me—I like honesty even if it ruffles some feathers."

"Ms. McIntyre." He paused. "I don't think my personal life has anything to do with my wrangling experience. Just to be clear, *she* stayed on, and I thought it best to move along."

"Sorry it didn't work out," I said.

"Me too. If it helps my case, I'd think I'd still be there if it had." He leaned forward with rounded shoulders. "I've never had an interview while riding."

"We like to do things differently around here. Figured y'all would be more relaxed on the back of your best ride." I wrapped my hand in Gypsy's mane as we trotted up the steepest part of the incline. I waited at the top and watched Silas ride. I rubbed my belly, grateful for the easy feeling this morning.

Silas strayed from the trail to get Huckleberry from beyond the dense pines. "I can play your game, little lady." He circled her and shooed her toward the path.

I approved of the tone he took with the first girl I'd ever ridden. Her gray whiskers twitched as she held my gaze. "That's Silas. He doesn't mean any harm. Now get going, Berry."

Silas rode over. He eyed Cora and Big Red. "You've got some beauties."

"We sure do." I scanned the hillside for the lingerers and pointed toward Tristan's charge, Casanova. "That one with the ice-blue eyes is beautiful. Likes to get the others riled up though. He's the wildcard in the bunch and belongs to Tristan," I said.

Casanova's ears went back, and he trotted away. Before I could ride toward him, Tristan emerged from the tree line. Casanova reared up with a squeal.

Tristan's easy strides and instincts came naturally. His sharp whistle produced three more mares from the shadows. He rode up to the ridge and circled around. Silas joined him. The two worked together to round up the rest. Gypsy and I made our way down the slope and into the clearing. Dad and Levi worked the growing herd of antsy horses ready to run.

Tristan was down the mountain and by my side in a quick clip.

"Where's Silas?"

"Wait for it," Tristan said.

"What the heck?" I pushed my hat back from my brow. Silas appeared to be the Pied Piper of equine.

"And look who's following on his heels." Tristan's deep tone was almost a growl.

"My sweet Huckleberry. Dang. She's always the last one. How'd he get 'em in orderly fashion? I've never seen anything like this before."

"He's singing to them. Listen," Tristan said.

I tugged my hat down low. My gaze met Matt's as he and Trigger trotted over. "Hey, cowboy. Check it out."

"That's some voice." He nodded and gave Trout the high sign to open the gate. Slow gaits eased into full canters, and we followed. Tristan rode ahead with Silas on his heels. Levi stayed close to Dad on the outside of the herd and rode at a slower pace. Matt and I brought up the rear with Trout.

"Levi seems to be playing a part. I'm not so sure he's cowboy material," Trout said. "As Ida May used to say, 'He may be all hat and no cattle.'"

I laughed. "We'll find out, won't we?"

Matt pushed his shoulders back. "He sure does have a fancy saddle for a kid who wants to find himself."

"Did he tell you that? I'm not sure this job is about *finding yourself*," I said.

"Maybe not, but many of us do, don't we?" Matt rubbed his chin. "Didn't we, Trigger?"

Trigger whinnied and shook his head. Matt gave his speckled chestnut a nudge with his boot heels, and they rode ahead.

"The boy's got a good head on his shoulders.

You'd do well to follow his lead," Trout said.

"I'm not sure I'm the following kind of gal unless I'm dancing, and even then, it's a toss-up."

"Being a leader don't mean you have to be the head honcho."

My gaze met Trout's. "So you know about Dad's offer to Matt."

"Yep."

I waited for Trout to weigh in. "You gonna say anything else?" I asked.

"Nope." He shut the gate and locked it.

"Well then. You ready to ride home, cowboy?"

Trout nodded. "Wanna race?"

"Nope. Two can play your game. It's time I hang back for once. You've got a mighty different perspective bringing up the rear."

CHAPTER 13

MAGGIE HAD MADE a heap of bacon, eggs, oatmeal, and fruit salad for breakfast. Afterward, we all helped clear the table. Levi and Silas had chipped in cheerfully, certainly not shy of compliments to the chef and her cheerful disposition. Dad pulled me aside before we left the house.

"Is this panning out like you thought?" he asked.

"I guess so. I've never done this before." I held his stare. "Tristan is Tristan. He seems to like to handle things on his own. Not sure what he's thinking half the time. Silas is great. Cooperative, friendly, and strong. That's for sure. But what's the deal with Levi? He's kind of skittish for a wrangler, and he's glued to your side."

"Not sure if he's comfortable with a herd of animals. Seems nice enough."

"Nice is fine, but not exactly what we're looking for," I said.

"Remember that when you're picking at Tristan." Dad buttoned his jacket. "For the life of me,

I don't see why he rubs you the wrong way." He scratched his chin. "Could it be you're more like him than you'd like to be? Looking in the mirror is easy. Accepting what you see is the hard part."

"Dang, Dad. Didn't know I was gonna get a come-to-Jesus talk today. Apparently, you and Matt have been talking about more than ranching and new prospects. I should be included."

Dad crossed his arms over his chest. "Just making a case to keep the boy on."

"Not to mention, reminding me that I'm difficult." I tucked my hands in my pockets.

"Take it how you want, sweetheart. If you want a stronger voice around here, you gotta be fair. Look at the whole picture. Think about the trees beyond the forest."

"Will that get me an offer to be your co-CEO?"

Dad sighed. "That's not on the table. There's more to running this place than doing the paperwork, keeping a ledger, buying equipment and stock. You know that. I know you want to be my co-CEO. This ranch is as much yours as it is mine." He paused. "To be honest, Matt's background in business is a better fit for the position."

My mind reeled. Holding the position would ensure my input even if I got sidetracked raising a child. When it was my turn to inherit the ranch, I wanted a clear picture of the job ahead and past practice, not to mention a voice those working for me would respect. I hadn't watched my grandpa and my dad all these years to get left behind now. Being involved in every aspect, every decision, would only strengthen my ability to carry on the legacy I prided myself on.

"Dad—" He rested his fingers on my lips.

"Before you go off, you get those cattle and horses in line without blowing your top or being harsh. You're up every morning, saddling the horses, keeping them healthy, making schedules, organizing the barn, and waiting for the sun to show you a new day. I don't know if you're following me or not, but wouldn't you be happier *not* being behind the scenes? That boy doesn't want to wear a suit and sit in an office building, but his business sense is on-target. I thought the opportunity would help him find his way without leaving what's important to him."

"Like you did when you decided to become a pediatrician?"

"Yes, like I did. Just thought I could save everyone some time and heartache."

I tucked hair behind my ears and digested his words. "I thought I had to make my own mistakes." Dad slid his finger beneath my chin and lifted my gaze.

"You've been working awfully hard to be assertive, Chloe. And yes, we all need to learn lessons in our own ways. You've got plenty of mistakes and lessons ahead of you. We all do. I'm just trying to help. It's not that I don't want you to be co-CEO. As owner, I want what's best for this place, and that means you...in the long run. Ida May would call that tough love."

I looked into my father's eyes. The crow's feet had crept into his temples and multiplied. The gray in his beard shimmered a little brighter. His heart was invested in the things that made him tick. Time didn't change what mattered most. There were a lot of what-ifs floating through my mind, but now wasn't the time to air them. We had business to do.

"You gonna say anything?" he asked.

"Will anything I say change your mind?" Dad shook his head, so I rolled up my sleeves and put on my hat. "We better get going before those cowboys start sloughing off. We can chat along the way. It's time to saddle up." I opened the mudroom door and ushered Dad out.

We hadn't gone far when we found Levi sitting on the boulder by the stream, chewing on a stalk of grass. Dad patted him on the back. "Come on, son, we've got some cattle to tend to."

MATT, TROUT, DAD, and I rode out to the north pasture with Tristan, Silas, and Levi. Justin and Quinn stayed behind to work with the horses and clean up the odds and ends we'd let simmer.

The blue sky overhead swallowed us as we rode away from the ranch, each finding our own paths across the valley. The quiet space between us made for idle conversation. When Dad's ride was interrupted, Gypsy and I were there to relieve him from Levi's company.

"Dad, Matt's got something he wants to run by you. Levi and I can manage." I waited for Dad to get out of earshot. "So, Levi. How do you feel about handling a chain saw or roping a bull?" He didn't answer, so I continued. "How would you go about retrieving cattle from a flooded ditch or the mud?"

He tugged at his supple leather hat detailed with a hatband of buffalo nickel medallions. I inspected his boots for signs of wear and labor.

"You've got an impressive application. I hear you're looking for an opportunity to find your calling. Wrangling is more than a calling. It's a way of life. I suspect you already know that though," I said.

"I thought I'd be riding with your father."

"Thought you might like to spend time with me, too. And by the way, nice job this morning." I shooed away the buzzing near my ear. "This afternoon, we're gonna get dirty. Can't wait to see y'all throw a rope and troubleshoot."

Levi rode quietly. "The landscape sure is beautiful. Amazing how different parts of the country have their own characteristics."

"Where'd you grow up?" I swayed to Gypsy's easy gait.

"Napa Valley," he answered.

"I hear Napa's a beautiful place. Remind me where you went to college." I ran my fingers through Gypsy's mane.

"Went to University Cal-Davis. After I graduated, I went to Italy for two years, then moved back to Cali." His voice trailed off. "Started working for my father."

"What's your father do?"

He hesitated. "My family owns a vineyard in Napa Valley. Have you ever heard of—?"

"Don't tell me now," I interrupted. "We can talk about family over a game of horseshoes after dinner if you're up to it." I pulled back on my reins. "That explains Italy."

He nodded. "My father sent me to study in Tuscany."

"What'd you say you have a degree in?" I glanced at him.

"Agriculture business—but it's actually in viti-culture." He fiddled with his reins. "Is my interview over?" Tattoo lowered his gaze as if he knew Levi had been exposed, too.

"Do you want it to be over?"

"No, ma'am." Levi sat taller in his big-ticket saddle tooled with intricate design and impeccable buckstitching.

"Then it's not over." I nudged Gypsy to move along. "Is Tattoo *really* your horse?"

"Yep. My father loves grapes. I love horses. If we're being honest, I can hold my own when it comes to making wine, too. My father thinks I'm being foolish trying my hand at wrangling."

"You ever run a chain saw or get a cow out of the mud?"

He shook his head. "I was the captain of the equestrian team."

"So why are you in Montana?" I asked.

"Just making sure I don't belong anywhere else than Napa. I've already ruled out Texas, Colorado, and Oregon. Montana's my last stop."

"How many horses do you have back home?"

"Thirteen," he answered. "My family has a stable on the vineyard property."

"Are all your horses as well-bred as Tattoo?"

"Yes, ma'am."

I tipped my hat to Levi. "Come on, I've got a few things to show you, cowboy. I won't out you in front of the others. If you want to come clean, that's on you."

"Thank you, ma'am."

Gypsy and I trotted ahead, and Levi followed.

THE SEVEN OF us converged into a united posse when the cattle came into view. "I'll make a sweep along stream. Any takers?" I looked at Levi, hoping he'd follow.

"We'll all go," Dad said.

I nudged Gypsy into an easy trot, and off we went. The sound of galloping hooves made my blood race. I couldn't fathom not riding even if for a little while. I'd enjoy this time until the doctor said otherwise. The clouds rolling in brought a subtle breeze that prickled the back of my neck. I slowed up and let our visitors take the lead with Tristan. If nothing else, he was proving to be a great guide while the rest of us hung back and watched the potential wranglers operate.

Tristan, Silas, and Levi had stopped near the calves wading in the stream. The cloud of dust they created billowed to the east. Trout and I meandered closer. We'd talked about testing the wranglers' skills further before heading out, and the timing seemed right. "Let's see what Tristan and Levi can do about this situation. Suppose these two calves needed some help getting out of the water. How would you work as a team?"

Tristan, Levi, and Silas dismounted their horses.

"Silas, could you hold the horses while Tristan and Levi work? And be thinking about what you'll do in a minute."

"Sure thing, Ms. McIntyre." His round cheeks and full beard framed his smile.

Tristan took the lead; Levi followed. "If they were really stuck"—Tristan shot me a look, and his brow read irritated—"I'd rope them and pull and let Levi push from the rear."

"I'm good with that," Levi said.

"Let's see it." I gestured for Tristan and Levi to execute the plan. The first calf cooperated with the charade. The second calf wandered downstream. I dismounted Gypsy and took the reins from Silas. "Now let's see how you round up number two, who's heading the wrong way. Don't forget your rope."

"With all due respect, Ms. McIntyre, I don't need a rope," Silas said.

I anticipated he'd break into song like he'd done this morning. He walked along the stream, whistling a mellow tune. When the calf settled in his presence, he stepped into the shallow water, picked up the calf, and carried her to dry ground.

Trout bowed his head and snickered. "Well done. Not what I expected, but bravo," I said. The calf peered at Silas, then rubbed her nose against his chaps. Tristan planted his hands on his hips and dropped his chin to the ground.

"I'd use a rope if I needed to. Just figured up close and personal gets me a little more respect when we meet again."

Tristan mounted Hitch in a huff while Levi assessed his wet boots when he thought no one was looking. Silas unbuttoned and shed his jacket to reveal a plain black tee that hugged his ripped chest. Defined muscles flexed in his arms as he tucked his denim in Cisco's saddlebag.

"Shall we move along?" I handed Levi Tattoo's reins, and Silas saddled up. "Dad, what do you have in mind?"

"Let's say we break into pairs. I'll take Levi with me," he said.

"How about I take Tristan? Silas, you go with

Matt. It'll give you two a chance to chat. Trout, which way you headed?"

"I'll ride solo." He gave a quick nod. With a swift jerk of the reins, he and Tupelo Honey were headed for the horizon.

Tristan and Hitch paced. Tristan watched the other riders leave one by one. I waved for him to follow me.

"You are something else." He shifted his weight in the saddle.

"Hey. I thought you said you were on your best behavior today."

"I didn't need Levi's help getting the calf out of the stream."

"Just thought you and Levi could work together." I pushed my hat back from my brow and held his disgusted stare.

Tristan dismounted Hitch, looked him in the eye, and told him to stay put. Tristan walked over to the calf he and Levi had retrieved from the stream. He picked her up, carried her back into the water, and set her down. Then he marched back over to get the second calf, picked her up, carried her into the stream, and set her down. "Are there any others you'd like me to move for you? That water ain't nothing but a trickle this time of year."

"No thanks." Gypsy and I circled him. "You

know if you pick them up too many times, they'll be wanting you to carry them all the time."

"I don't know what I did to you, but this is—" Tristan's chest rose and fell with a deep breath. "What it is." He knelt beside the stream and splashed his blossoming cheeks with water. "We should get going," he said, getting back into the saddle.

Hitch and Gypsy stood nose to nose.

"Yes, we should. I wouldn't want anyone thinking I was giving you special treatment." I pushed his buttons as much as he pushed mine.

Tristan gestured for me to lead the way.

CHAPTER 14

AFTER A QUICK lunch, Matt and I went to the appointment with Dr. Hennessey. Nothing had been out of the ordinary except Matt's presence. My paper gown left me feeling exposed and less than attractive, but Dr. Hennessey's caring bedside manner calmed the river of anxiousness rolling through me. She'd confirmed I could continue riding after Matt aired his concerns and asked his laundry list of questions. She even showed him her bulletin board in her office covered with pictures of newborns and pregnant women on their horses.

Mountains lined both sides of the winding road back to the ranch. Getting lost in the familiar scenery overshadowed the butterflies returning to my stomach. I opened my window. The sound of the river was better than any over-the-counter medicine. I pressed my back against the leather seat and swept away the hair stuck in my eyelashes. Scented strands of sage, wildflowers, dust, and water in the air centered me.

Matt put his hand on top of mine.

"You okay?" he asked. "The doctor said everything was normal."

"I'm fine." My heart raced. I reached over and put his hand on my chest.

He wiggled his fingers until they were inside the buttons of my cotton shirt. "Holy cow, girl."

"Today made it all real. We're going to be parents, Matt Cooper. You and me. Together. And we have a due date. May 22."

Matt turned into the drive. We drove under the timber gateway marking the 617 Ranch. Pine trees dotted the long road back to the house. The truck bumped over the bridge and across the river running through our property.

"Thanks for going with me." I covered his hand, still resting on my chest.

"You're welcome," he said. "I've told you before, you won't be alone."

"Great, then can you gain the extra weight and have the sore boobs coming my way? I should let you know, the list is long, but I'll save it for some other time."

"If I could, I would." He parked the truck and pointed to the house.

I released my seat belt, pushed the door open, and ran onto the porch to welcome Glad. She was seated in Grandpa's rocking chair. The shimmer of her strawberry-red hair in the sunlight dominated the sparse tresses of silver. She stood with open arms, and I melted into her.

"Oh my goodness," she squealed. "Here's my beauty. Let me get a good look at you."

She put her hands on my waist and leaned back. I wiped the corners of my eyes as her green gaze skimmed over me. "You're shorter," I said to lighten the moment.

"And you're just as sassy," she replied. "What's with the scarf on your head? You look like one of those crazy rock stars."

I laughed. "I wish." Matt shuffled up the stairs. "This is Matt Cooper. Matt Cooper, this is Glad Abernathy, Maggie's mom."

Glad reached to shake his hand.

"Ma'am, no offense, but that's not how we greet family around here." He took her hand in his and kissed her on the cheek. "Nice to finally meet you. I've heard a lot of great things about you. Ate plenty of those delicious homemade cookies you used to send Chloe at school."

Glad reveled in the greeting, her cheeks pinker than blooming primrose. "He's a keeper, in case you're wondering," she said.

"Yeah, he's a good guy." I tucked my hands in

my pockets.

"Well, if you ladies don't mind, I have some chores to get back to, and I'm sure you have plenty of catching up to do. Chloe, we'll talk about Silas, Levi, and Tristan later." Matt excused himself with a dimpled wink.

I pulled Glad close. "How was your trip? It's been too long."

"Goodness, child." Her voice cracked. "It was very comfortable. I had a first-class ticket and doting flight attendants. Apparently, they think being eighty-eight makes me fragile. I'm just getting started. Doctor says I'm fit as a fiddle."

Glad's age didn't matter. I didn't believe she was a number any more than the rest of us. I figured I'd be young forever, and that's how I liked to envision the people I loved. "Well, you look fabulous in your jeans and plaid blouse."

She pointed to her feet. "And the boots. Giddy up, cowboy." She held up her hands. "My fingers may be a bit gnarled, but my mind is sharp."

"Must be from all the knitting." I hooked my arm in hers. "Where are the others? Did they leave you out here for the bears?"

"Now, don't go getting after them. I insisted on sitting outside and waiting for you." Glad closed her eyes and inhaled. "I forgot how sweet the air smells here." Her smile stretched from cheek to cheek.

"Shall we go inside and see what they're up to?" I hugged her again. "I'm so glad you're here."

"Me too, sweet girl," she said, patting my hand.

Glad held the doorframe and stepped inside. My mind flooded with memories. Glad was my human bandage. She had bent the rules, making life bearable when I had struggled. She'd taught me that dreams evolve and come in batches like baked goods and all things sweet dusted in sugar.

"Sure does smell good in here," she said, sniffing the air.

"Maggie's making barbeque. What do you say we see what she's up to?"

Glad and I made our way into the kitchen and sat at the counter. Maggie poured salad dressing on the cabbage slaw. She stirred, tasted then handed her mom a spoonful.

"Perfect," Glad said.

"How soon until dinner?"

"About thirty minutes," Maggie answered.

Glad watched me intently. Her stare bounced from Maggie to me and back.

"What is it? Do I have something on my face?"

Glad shook her head. "No, dear."

I stood and walked to the other side of the counter. I found the jar of smoked almonds and poured them into a glass bowl. "So tell me what you're knitting these days."

"I haven't done any complicated patterns lately. I'm making potholders for the church bazaar and, of course, beanies for the babies at the hospital. Made a cable scarf not too long ago. Just takes me a little longer than it used to."

"I still have the purple beanie you knitted me. Remember it?"

"How could I forget? I made one for your little friend, too. What was her name?"

"Lily," I answered. "We chat on social media sometimes."

"It's nice you're still friends." Glad fidgeted with the gold band she wore on her ring finger.

I opened the refrigerator, took out the pitcher of lemonade, then shut the door. Glad's ogling stare over the rim of her glasses was inescapable.

"Okay, what?"

She cleared her throat. "So tell me about this Matt fellow who dropped you off."

"What's there to tell? We met at Montana State. We've been friends for about seven years. He works with us on the ranch. He's a great guy."

"And?" Glad beckoned. "Seven years is a long

time to know each other. Interesting.”

Maggie smiled.

“You two”—I pointed to Glad then Maggie—“are creeping me out.”

Maggie sliced up strawberries for the fruit salad. “Chloe, Glad has requested to be your roommate while she’s here.”

Glad pushed her glasses to the top of her head.

“Excellent,” I said with a hard swallow. “A girl doesn’t have two double beds in her room for nothing.”

DINNER HAD TASTED delicious going down. But now I slumped over the toilet, holding my hair back with one hand and bracing myself against the cold porcelain with the other. The baby did not like barbeque. My nose burned. My eyes watered.

There was a knock at the door.

The knock came again. Then Matt spoke up.

A pain slithered through my back as I got to my feet. I inspected my bloodshot stare in the mirror and splashed cold water on my face. I opened the door a crack and peered out.

Matt leaned close. “Are you okay?”

“I’ll be fine. I need a minute.”

“You don’t appear to be fine, and I saw the

look on your face before you left the table."

"The barbeque upset my stomach."

Matt shook his head. "Are you coming back to join us, or will you be getting ready for bed early?"

The next wave of nausea washed over me. I hurried back to the toilet. Matt's boot heels clicked against the tile floor. He held my hair back and caressed my arm as I gripped the toilet.

"I'm sorry you're sick."

I stood, and he handed me a wet washcloth. "Stop apologizing. That doesn't make it any better."

"I wish there were something I could do to help."

"Sometimes there's nothing anybody can do to make an uncomfortable situation better. This aversion to food will pass like any given nightmare." I was sure my breath smelled of vomit and my eyes were the color of a Bloody Mary. I tucked loose strands of hair behind my ears.

Matt put his arm around me, regardless.

"I'll say this again. I won't let you go through this alone," he said.

My stomach clenched and cramped. "Please, don't say anything or move." I leaned against the wall to steady myself.

Worry pinched at the corners of Matt's eyes

while I pretended the waves of nausea didn't exist.

"This is like the time I ate all my Halloween candy in one night," I said, closing the lid to sit down. Matt knelt beside me. "Who knew pregnancy would be the gift that keeps on giving *before* the baby comes?" My joke was met with silence.

"You ate all your Halloween candy all in one night?"

"Yes, and it wasn't a well-thought-out plan," I said.

"Man, Chloe, what did you think would happen?"

"I don't know. Everything tasted so good. I was so sick, I missed two days of school."

Matt bowed his head. His shoulders shook with laughter.

I swatted him again and stood. "Get out of here." He exited the bathroom, shaking his head. I rolled my eyes and shut the door.

I sat back down on the toilet and held my head in my hands. There was another knock on the door. "I'll be fine. I promise. I need another minute."

Glad opened the door and poked her head in, her curious nature still untamed.

"Sorry about the tone." I folded the cool washcloth and placed it on my forehead. "I thought you were Matt."

"Apparently," she uttered under her breath.

"Do you need to use the bathroom? I'm almost done."

"No, dear. I looked up from my plate and you were gone. Just came to check on you."

"You're sweet." I stood and patted my cheeks. "You're not catching me at my finest moment. Dinner didn't quite agree with me."

"I'll wait in the hallway for you."

I shut the door, took a deep breath, washed up, and opened the door. She waited with crossed arms and a questioning stance like Maggie would.

"I don't know why you can't come out and tell me. You used to share everything," she said.

"Tell you what?" I asked.

"That you're pregnant." Glad rested her hand on my arm.

"Did Maggie tell you?"

"No," she said.

"How did you know?" I'd never known her to have the sixth sense of a bloodhound like her daughter. I leaned against the wall.

Glad shrugged.

"Did Tristan tell you?"

"No. But he seems like a nice fellow. Awfully quiet at dinner. Handsome, though. Those other fellows are good-looking as well. No eyesores around here. That's for sure."

"Then who? Dad, Maggie?"

"Some secrets are best left a secret."

"It was Maggie, wasn't it?" I pressed.

Glad twiddled her thumbs. "I wasn't sure when I heard the words, but you were the only one I could think of who might be with child."

I shook my head. "Huh?"

"You're gonna think this is crazy, but my knitting group went to see the psychic woman with the red beehive from New York. I love that charm bracelet she wears, and her snazzy wardrobe is to die for. Anyway, she pointed me out in the audience. My friend Lois got front row tickets. She said we had to go. She watches the show every week."

"You're making this up," I said.

"No, I'm not. Cross my heart, hope to die, stick a needle in my eye."

"You remember the oath," I said. "You get points for that."

"She said something to me about mountains and new life. That there was a baby in my future."

"Seriously?" I scrunched up my face at her.

"Yes, seriously. I called Bradley, but he said it wasn't him. Maggie certainly isn't having a baby, and that leaves only you." Glad rubbed my belly.

"I don't believe you," I said.

She raised her brows and turned her palms to the ceiling. "Fine, but if Maggie asks, I tried my best to keep my mouth shut."

"I knew it."

"Really? You didn't believe me...at all?"

"Maybe a little bit when you said your friend Lois had tickets. And the part about Lois saying you needed to see the show. Do you even belong to a knitting group?"

"Yes. Great bunch of gals. Lois, she's a hoot, especially when she's had a couple of glasses of wine."

"I've missed you, Gladiola." I held her hands in mine. "Did you *really* see the psychic?"

"Sure did. We sat in the balcony though. Didn't even get close to the woman. Tickets went like hotcakes." Glad patted my arm. "You feel like coming back outside?"

"I'm going to get some ginger ale first. Anyone start the fire yet?"

"They were working on it when I came inside. Maggie said something about s'mores."

I grimaced and held my stomach. "I'll pass." Glad put her arm around my waist. "You're definitely getting shorter," I joked. The fine lines around her eyes mapped her good nature.

"I suppose I am." She tugged at the hem of her blouse and squared her shoulders. "Just means the love is more compact."

"I was going to tell you. Thought maybe my news was something I shouldn't lead with," I said.

"Kid, with me, you can lead with anything. As long as it's not one of your right hooks," she teased.

"Yeah, those tend to get me into trouble." I draped my arm around her shoulder.

Glad and I returned to the party; she sipped her wine, and I savored my ginger ale. I sat next to Dad, then smiled at Matt, letting him know everything was cool. I put my feet up on the log, leaned back, fixated on the sky, and listened to the hum of conversation. Dad patted my hand.

"Will you play a tune for me, Dad?"

He strummed the guitar and played as well as Grandpa used to. Dad was all the things his father was: strong, brave, tough as nails on the outside, and soft on the inside when he needed to be.

"This cowboy song is one I remember my momma singing. Wish you could've seen her ride," Dad said. "She could fix a fence, cow punch, and keep me in line. Just like you, sweetheart. Taught Trout a thing or two." Pride sparked his gaze.

Maggie squeezed my hand. My insides turned over and not from food aversion or morning sickness. Matt took off his hat and set it on the bench next to him, then ran his hand through his hair. His dark gaze was as rich as the evening light spilling over the mountaintops.

I made a wish upon the stars, like I did every night.

"Make it a good one," Maggie said.

"I will."

CHAPTER 15

SILAS AND LEVI helped round up the horses at dawn. Quinn had stayed close to Levi. By the time they rode in, Levi sounded like one of the guys, and I was beginning to think he could wrangle, in time.

Tristan drove up as the last horses ran into the corral. I dismounted Gypsy and met him in the drive. "Dad said you found some strays this morning. How come you didn't put them in the pen?"

He shut the truck door. "Figured if they got out, there might be more lingering near the road. Didn't want to disturb anyone, so I loaded them up and took 'em back, found a clogged ditch and fixed it up." He gestured to the trailer. "Figured Silas and Levi could handle the morning roundup."

"It's okay to disturb me. I wouldn't mind. In fact, I'd prefer it."

"Good to know. I would've called if I needed help." Tristan unloaded the tools from the truck bed and headed for the shed.

"I really wouldn't have minded," I said to myself.

"You talking to yourself again." Justin snatched the pickax from the truck and followed his brother.

I went around the back of the barn to the corral, my chin to the ground. Tristan ran past, and I looked up to see what the rush was. The back quadrant of the corral had flooded, and Butch and Sundance were rolling in the mud like a couple of hogs.

I ran to the water spigot.

Tristan wiggled through the rails and yelled for Quinn to open the gate to the adjoining pasture. Justin scooted through the fence and shooed the herd toward the pond. Mud soaked my denim. Just as I reached for the knob, I lost my footing and fell to my knees. I braced myself on the fence, leaning toward the shut off valve. Trying to find my footing was like trying to navigate black ice. My boots sunk into the ground. I stretched, had my fingers on the knob, and went down again.

Silas came from behind and turned off the water.

"What is going on?" I got to my knees.

"Before I went to bed, I came out to fill up the trough with fresh water. Guess I got sidetracked when my phone rang," he said.

I inspected my mud-covered hands and reached out to him. "Must've been important."

The apples of his cheeks turned pink. "I should've waited to call her back. I hope being honest gets me a brownie point or two. Thought I'd save you some time investigating."

"I appreciate your efforts." I grabbed onto his fingers and pulled myself up. "My feet are stuck."

"No worries, Ms. McIntyre. I gotcha."

Before I knew it, Silas plucked me from the muddy pool and plopped me over his shoulder like a sack of potatoes.

Justin wasn't even attempting to hide his grin on the sidelines. "Look on the bright side. Only six of them went for a beauty bath."

Silas set me down. I shook off my hands and hung my hat on the fence post. "I should get cleaned up. I'm dripping."

"I'll take care of the mess, Ms. McIntyre."

Dad joined us. "Leave 'em be, son. You can bathe the horses after they've had their fun and the ground dries. Might not be for a bit."

"Sorry, sir. This is my fault."

I waved him off. "Not necessary to go any further." Tristan handed me the bandana from his back pocket. I wiped my hands, then handed it to Justin.

"You missed a spot, bosslady," he said, rubbing my chin with his thumb.

I rested my hands on his shoulders and held his gaze. "Thank you, cowboy."

"My pleasure." He draped the muddy bandana over the fence. "Bet Silas will give you a piggyback ride to the house or the nearest car wash."

I put my hand on Silas's chest before he could pick me up again. "He's kidding. I'm good."

"You sure? You're light as a feather," Silas said.

"Really. It's okay. I'm sure my dad has something better for you to do."

"On that cue, men, we should let my daughter get cleaned up." Dad shooed Justin and Silas away. "Nice job with the strays this morning, Tristan. I appreciate your hard work."

"You're welcome, sir."

I nodded and walked away. Levi waited at the barn door, watching the scene unfold.

I waved him off before he could say anything. "Everything is okay, Levi. It might take me awhile to get cleaned up."

Tristan waltzed into the barn with a bridle in one hand and a branding iron in the other.

"Where'd you get that? You know we use tags." I shut the office door.

"Found it in the rafters." Tristan pointed overhead. "It's a great piece of history. Thought I'd bring it down."

"What were you doing up there?"

"Man, you sure do have a lot of questions."

I rested my hands on my hips. "Seriously, what were you doing up there?"

"I heard something rustling around. Thought I'd check for critters. Only a bird hunting for nesting ground. It flew away as soon as I started moving things around."

I turned my back to him and brushed Huckleberry.

"Why are you upset with me now? I wasn't the one who caused the mud slick," he said.

I didn't say anything. I continued grooming my freckled friend. Her coat was as shiny as the day I met her.

Tristan came closer. I studied his scuffed boots, worn as mine.

"Seriously, why the cold shoulder? I already apologized," he said.

I stroked Huckleberry's rump. "You're not much like your brother." His presence prickled my nerves.

"I hear that sentiment a lot."

Huckleberry's snout found my belly. When she shifted her weight, I moved out of the way, cautious not to get my feet caught beneath her hooves. Tristan held me steady.

"Careful now, you're carrying precious goods."

"You're so inappropriate." My tone matched the intensity of his stare.

"I didn't mean to be inappropriate. I don't want you to get hurt." He paused. "And you should know, I'm not here to irritate you or take anything away from you. I'm here to work and earn a paycheck. I've been wrangling since I was a teenager. Never had anything like you do."

"What's that supposed to mean?"

Tristan put his hands up in surrender. "I'm just saying, I think you're pretty lucky."

"It's more than luck. Everyone works hard around here, including me."

"Won't that change soon?"

I tossed the brush in the tack box, turned on a heel, and left. I kicked up dirt in my path. What was wrong with him? I tugged at the front of my cowboy hat and put my head down.

Tristan scurried behind me. He caught my arm, and I swung around. His leather glove was rough against my skin. I jerked away. "Nothing has been easy for me either, so please don't make rash assumptions. You know nothing about me."

"Chloe," he said.

"What?"

"Nothing," he said.

"You may as well say it." My challenge was met with a stern expression and a twitching left temple.

I tucked my fingers in my back pockets and lifted my chin. He took off his gloves and squeezed them with a tight fist. I turned on a heel and walked away.

I SLAMMED THE mudroom door and stomped into the kitchen. I pushed my hat back from my forehead and peered into the refrigerator.

"What's all the racket?" Glad asked.

I shut the refrigerator door so hard, the glass containers rattled. "Sorry," I said. "Guess I'm a little worked up."

"About what?"

I pulled out a stool for her to sit on. She hiked herself up and leaned on the counter. I grabbed an apple from the bowl and bit into it. Juice squirted in my eye, and I rubbed away the sting. "That Tristan is so annoying." Glad sat quietly and inspected me from head to toe.

"Maybe he likes you."

"I doubt it. And anyone claiming a guy likes you because he's inconsiderate is full of bull hockey."

"So what's his problem?" Glad's forehead wrinkled like a country map.

"I don't know."

Dad came into the kitchen and sat down beside Glad. He set his hat on the counter, his scowl directed toward me. I took another bite of my apple, the brittle snap quick and intentional. Glad excused herself.

"I drove out to the north field to check the fence. The barn's cleaned up," I said.

"I'm just going to get to the point. Tristan says you two had words. The boy has no clue why you clash."

"I'm not going to defend myself, because if I do, it'll look like I did something wrong, and I didn't do anything wrong. He doesn't like women ranchers, and if he's going to stay around here, he better get used to it. Silas and Levi don't seem to have a problem with me." I bit off another chunk of apple and stared at my dad.

He rubbed his temples.

I chewed then swallowed.

"Are you listening to yourself? That makes no sense." Dad groaned.

I tossed my almost finished apple into the sink. It landed with a thud.

"Chloe, you agreed we need another set of hands. He might be rough around the edges, but he means well."

"He might mean well, but he doesn't have to remind me I'm having a baby or that my role around here won't exactly be the same after I do."

"This can't continue," Dad said. "Seems to me you haven't quite accepted the inevitable. Just because someone addresses the baby doesn't mean they're knocking you down a peg. We have business to do, and business doesn't involve a strongheaded woman and the potential new guy butting heads on a regular basis."

"Who says he's the new guy?"

"Chloe, we've both seen all we need to see from our three candidates. The decision can be made tomorrow," Dad said.

Maggie came into the kitchen. "Sounds like a serious discussion."

I leaned against the counter. The button on my jeans poked my belly. How much longer would I fit into my pants, let alone after the baby came? Finding pants that fit would be easier than admitting Dad had a point. "The look on your face tells me you've already made your decision."

"The boy's trying to do the right thing. He's got two left feet when it comes to communicating sometimes." Dad stood, put his hat on, and tugged it tight against his forehead. "And, Chloe, being someone's boss doesn't give you the right to be unreasonable. Those young men out there"—he pointed out the window—"are seeking work. Our job is to choose the best man for our team. And if we're being honest, I know who you think is the best man to fill the position."

When I wished upon the stars tonight, I'd asked for the strength to admit to myself and my father that he was right about Tristan. Tristan's drive was 617 worthy. In time, Tristan's biting edge that felt like the north wind blowing through would fade into the horizon like the day's end if I let it.

Glad poked her head around the corner. "Is it safe to come in?"

"Yes," I answered.

Dad exited through the mudroom.

Glad and Maggie joined me. Maggie got out her container of huckleberry ice cream and a spoon. "I'm tired. I've been working on organizing my photographs for hours. I didn't realize how many I had."

"Want a spoon?" I asked Glad.

"I'd love one. Sure looks good."

"I've eaten out of this container," Maggie said. "Bad habit. Chloe, you want to get Glad the guest carton? I always keep a spare."

"You sure are a funny girl. A few Maggie germs might do me good. Save your energy, Chloe. I'll eat out of my daughter's container. Let's save the dish soap."

"I'll have some of those Maggie germs, too. Might be good for the baby. Make her tough." I ate a spoonful and looked at the two ladies with high brows.

"I'm not so tough." Maggie paused to savor her bite of ice cream. "It's all in the delivery."

"She's right, you know. Others will eat out of your hand," Glad said. "Although it sounds like you've got a running start."

"Ha. Maybe the animals." I licked my spoon. "I suppose you heard my conversation with Dad."

"Yes," Maggie said.

"Good girl for standing your ground," Glad said.

"I don't think she needs *that* kind of support, Mom."

"Well, I beg to differ. There's nothing wrong with wanting to ranch and raise your own herd and do things your way." Glad beamed.

"I don't think I'll be having a herd," I said. "No thank you."

"Ain't nothing wrong with wanting a brood." Glad reached for the ice cream. "I've got to keep my energy up for my horse ride."

"Mom, you sure you want to get on a horse?" Concern lined Maggie's forehead.

"Look, I'm eighty-eight. It's on my bucket list," she said.

"When you put it that way…what Gladiola wants, Gladiola gets," Maggie said.

"Again, it's all in the delivery. I'm not going to ride through the meadow bareback and naked. I'm not gonna fall off with all these husky men around here. I want to ride a horse by the river and enjoy the land and the company."

"When you put it that way," I said. "I'll come along to make sure those *husky men* do their jobs."

"I'm looking forward to it." Glad cheered.

"Speaking of delivery." Maggie hurried off then returned with a package wrapped in brown paper.

I ran my fingers over my mother's return address. "Must be a belated birthday present."

"Open it," Glad said in the gentlest of tones.

"You know she's busy."

"She could've called. My birthday was more than a month ago." I turned the package over, took the pocketknife from Maggie, and opened the box. I set the cowboy boots on the counter. "She remembered my size." Copper, silver, and gunmetal studs covered the shafts. The distressed tan leather velvety to the touch. I opened the note.

Something extra special for my girl. Happy Birthday! Love, Mom.

"Those sure are fancy." Maggie picked up a boot and ran her fingers over the ornate design.

"Too fancy for slinging manure and working in the field."

"You going to call her and say thank you?" Glad asked.

I took a moment to think about my response. "I'll put a thank-you note in the mail tomorrow. I haven't told her about the baby, and the longer I wait, the better."

Maggie patted my shoulder. "We'll be here for you when you do," she said.

CHAPTER 16

Last night, I had laid awake thinking about Tristan and why he ruffled my mindset. Around midnight, a revelation occurred. He was a straight shooter, and his smarts about tending cattle and horses rivaled mine. His instincts provoked a vein of jealousy that made me question my authority and abilities. Before nodding off, I understood the only person I wanted challenging me was me.

Tristan shuffled around the barn with a handful of bridles. I watched his every move from the doorway, thinking about how to approach him. His profile was more mature and distinct than his brother's. Justin had told Dad that Tristan's wrangling skills surpassed the average Joe. Justin was honest about endorsing reputations, and I respected his opinion, despite my irrational clash with his brother.

Static on the radio jarred me, and I pulled the unit from the back of my belt to answer Matt's request for a pair of wire cutters. "Yeah, I got them. I'll throw the rest of tools in the truck and meet you out there." I signed off and hooked the radio back onto my belt.

Tristan stepped from the shadows. "What are you doing here? Spying on me? Thought you rode out with the rest of them."

The aroma of leather and disdain washed over me as I walked the plank-lined corridor of stalls and tack. "Nope. I'm driving the truck today." I rummaged through the toolbox, making sure I had the basics and that someone hadn't taken the pliers again. Besides Tristan, there wasn't anything more frustrating than missing tools.

I latched the top of the box, then carried it out to the truck. A fine mist floated through the air. Summer was my favorite time of year, and when it left, I mourned and counted the days until we'd meet again.

I shut the truck door and meandered back into the barn to grab a couple of shovels. Tristan stood in the doorway. My palms sweated. His prominent stare was hard to ignore.

Coal chased after me, mewing like she hadn't eaten in days. "Your round belly tells me you're not starving," I said. She jumped onto the tack box and mewed. "When I get back, I'll find you a snack." I scratched her ears, and she purred.

"The animals sure do like you," Tristan said, walking into the first stall.

"Yes, they do." I checked for my favorite pair of pliers in the toolbox before picking it up. "I'm not so sure you do, though."

"What makes you think I don't like you?" He poked his head out from behind the half door.

Coal scooted out of the barn. I picked out two of the best shovels and headed for the truck. Tristan followed me. The tip of the shovel in my right hand clunked against the plank floor.

"Seriously, what's with you?"

"What's with me?" I tossed the shovels in the bed of the truck, then secured the tailgate. "It's obvious you think I shouldn't be out there riding and doing half the things I'm doing. Or at least, that's how you come across. And you certainly do have some strong opinions about how things should be done around here." Antiquated, egocentric, and know-it-all came to mind.

"What do you have to prove anyway?" he asked.

"Plenty," I said.

"Not sure why. You're not going anywhere. It's the rest of us with something on the line." He relaxed his stance. "I happen to like it here and think this is where I belong, but then again, maybe

I'm kidding myself. Sure, Silas has potential, but he's not what this ranch needs. And Levi. He's a nice guy and all, but he knows his calling is elsewhere."

"I'm not the one you should be worried about," I told him. "My dad will have the final say."

"I beg to differ. I guess you don't realize the pull you have around here." A shadow washed over Tristan's dark stare.

"Look, this is not how I wanted this conversation to go, and Matt's waiting for me." I leaned against the truck and crossed my arms. The clouds rolled in faster than the morning stampede. I pulled my leather gloves from the back pocket of my jeans and wiggled my fingers into them. The gray sky brought an autumn chill that nipped at my nose, and I zipped up my oilcloth jacket.

Tristan checked the truck bed. "Don't go anywhere yet." He hustled back to the barn and returned with a pickax. "You might need this." He set it in the truck, then looked to the ominous sky. "You should think about getting a warmer jacket before you head out."

"I'll be fine." I got into the truck, closed the squeaky door, and rolled down the window. Tristan stood with his hands on his hips. "I'm not so bad," I told him.

"Never worked on a ranch like this before. I'm not sure what to make of the extraordinary cattle, let alone the stubborn woman who rides with fury across the fields and the idea of working alongside my competition."

"That's what makes us unique." I rolled up the window and started the engine.

I put my arm across the back of the seat and looked over my shoulder to avoid hitting the hitching post. I finished my three-point turn and shifted gears. Tristan's reflection held steady in my rearview mirror. A warm flash of heat prickled my nerves, and I drove away remembering Dad's words about being someone's boss.

The tires crunched along the gravel drive out to the main road. Even on a gray day, there wasn't anything finer than a herd of grazing horses and God's mountains surrounding our precious valley.

I gripped the steering wheel with both hands and focused on the road ahead. The river reflected the sky and appeared just as cold. Unexpected icy crystals melted on the windshield. Before long, they'd be sticking around.

I stopped at the end of the driveway. After checking for oncoming traffic, I turned left on the deserted two-lane highway. The shovels in the truck bed rattled as the rear tires moved over the uneven seam where the drive met the road. I turned on the wipers to clear the water spots skewing my vision. The static on the radio blared, then Dad called my name. I pulled over on the shoulder of the road to answer him.

"Hey, Dad. I just pulled out."

"I'd like Tristan to ride out with you. We've got some uncooperative heifers out here."

I rested my head against the cool window. "I'm sure Silas and Levi can handle them." I wiped away my foggy breath on the glass.

"Everyone gets a fair shot, Chloe. Get him out here. While I appreciate Levi's persistence, I'm not sure how many more calves Silas plans on physically moving. And to be honest, the singing is wearing on my nerves. Tristan is waiting for you."

"Fine. I'll go back and get him." I checked the rearview mirror, then cranked the steering wheel and headed back home.

"I could have been out in the field by now if I hadn't poked around the barn bantering. Dang it," I said to myself. As I accelerated, a sports car blared its horn, then swerved around me. I slammed on the brakes, my knuckles whiter than fresh snow. I hunched over the steering wheel, watching the silver blur disappear into the gray horizon.

The thought of being a fatality shook me. I loosened my grip and laid one hand on my belly. "Sorry about that, kid." A shiver ran through me. "I can feel Winston and Ida May, too." I gazed up to my special place on the ridge. "The view from there is more beautiful than a sanctuary gilded in gold and stained glass. I sure hope you like it here." For the first time, talking to the baby came naturally.

I checked my rearview mirrors, checked, and double-checked for vehicles before crossing the double yellow lines.

I pulled up to the barn. The fringe on Tristan's chaps swayed with each stride toward the truck. I leaned over and unlocked the passenger door. Tristan climbed in and buckled up. He set the insulated jacket I kept in the barn on the seat.

"Thanks for coming back to get me." He stared straight ahead, his chiseled profile angular and defined.

"Sure. Will you be needing a ride back?" I made my way to a place in the road where I could turn the truck around.

"Nope. They have a saddled horse ready and waiting for me."

I stopped at the end of the driveway, looked both ways, and hesitated before making the turn.

"Is something wrong?" Tristan asked.

"Just being overly cautious. Almost got hit a few minutes ago. I'm a bit shaky." My heart raced thinking about it.

"No cars my way. We're clear both ways," he said.

I pulled out and accelerated. The truck jerked forward.

"You want me to drive?"

"No thanks," I answered.

"Didn't think so, but I thought I'd ask."

I fidgeted in my seat. The sky moved quickly overhead. Tristan's stare warmed my cheeks, and my clammy hands gripped the wheel.

"I bet your heart stopped," Tristan said.

"What are you talking about?" I checked the mirrors and hugged the shoulder of the road until the oncoming semitruck passed.

"It's one thing to be by yourself when something life-threatening happens, but it's another when there's someone else involved."

His voice was deep, steady like the river's flow. He was right. Caution impeded my instincts. Caution prodded an uncharacteristic silence on my part. I wasn't ready to let Tristan know I agreed with him.

"You gonna ignore me all the way out to the pasture?"

I didn't answer.

"When there's a child involved, the stakes are grave," he said.

"How would you know?" I mumbled.

"Because I had a wife and a son, and I lost them both in a car accident."

Tristan's ominous tone made the hair stand up on the back of my neck. I eased up on the gas and tightened my grip on the steering wheel. Once again, he had rendered me speechless. My gaze met his, then went back to the open road. We neared the turn-off leading to the pasture where the cattle waited for us, where Dad rode with Matt and the others, where Tristan was supposed to be dropped off. I veered onto the cut-in and slowed down.

He watched me navigate the road and spoke to my father on the hand-held. I kept my head down. The rain had stopped. Tristan hopped out and waited for me to drive through the gate before shutting it. I watched him in the mirror until he got back in the truck.

"What happened to them?" I asked.

"A semi crossed over the yellow line. Hit the car my wife was driving. Killed them both instantly." Tristan's voice didn't waver.

I stared at him. My words stuck at the back of my throat. "I'm sorry. I had no idea."

"It's been two years and five months." Tristan's hard brow shaded his stormy gaze.

I couldn't take my eyes off him.

"Do you want me to drive?" he asked.

"No." I placed both hands on the steering wheel, then accelerated carefully to stay on the worn, earthy tracks we'd forged over the years.

I drew in a deep breath, trying to imagine the ache in his heart. "I've never known anyone with such tragedy," I said under my breath.

"Figured so," he said.

I peered across the open field ahead of us. Patches of blue appeared overhead among the streaks of gray and white. Sun beamed down like a Sunday message upon the open land. The sight lifted my mood and warmed me through before the shiver danced down my spine. Grandpa and Grandma weren't the only ones watching over us.

The truck bumped along the grassy terrain. "You must miss them something fierce," I said.

Cattle the color of winter grazed. Their muscular, angular bodies glowed in the light seeping down from above.

"This sight never gets old. They're beautiful," I said.

I stopped the truck not far from a stocky bull. His dark, irritated gaze held my attention. "He seems a bit ornery." I tried to hide the smile crossing my lips. The cattle weren't the only temperamental ones.

"Not so sure *ornery* is the right word. I interpret this cow's stare as curious, cautious of what's going on around him. See how he lifted his head?" Tristan explained. "Disposition really shouldn't be judged by a passing glance."

He got out, and the bull skittered away. If Tristan continued showing his soft side, accepting his flaws and forgiving his blunders would come more easily. In the deep breath I took, I understood why Matt and Dad thought Tristan and I had similar personalities. We both harbored hurt, strength, and a fierce determination to be the best while validating our efforts. Forging a working relationship with Tristan would not only benefit the ranch, but if I embraced the partnership, it would create opportunities to learn and grow.

"James would've loved being out here," Tristan said with a smile. "He would've been eight this year. Vivian would've been thirty-one. They both loved the land more than anything."

I leaned against the door. Tristan scanned the horizon until he saw Matt trotting across the field on one of our younger paints, Banshee, who had a love for running. Two horses ran alongside. I made eye contact with Gypsy. "I wondered where you'd gone." Her chocolate brown stare settled my rattled soul, and I suspected Tristan's, too.

Gypsy was saddled. Casanova fell in line, his studded halter a statement to his personality.

Tristan slipped on his leather gloves. "My ride awaits." Tristan whistled for his horse with the spooky demeanor. Casanova's crystal blue eyes shone bright in Tristan's presence.

"He's beautiful. The spots on his white hind end match the rest of him." He was lean and graceful. I knew the compliment wouldn't fix the rift I'd caused, but it was a start.

"Vivian was beautiful, too," he uttered under his breath. "Casanova was her favorite." Tristan glanced toward heaven. "Looks like you've got a ride, too."

Animals weren't any different than people. Spiritual connections ran deeper than a bottomless well and willed us to live. I stood beside a man who understood this premise as much as I did.

CHAPTER 17

MATT SLID THE reins over Gypsy's and Casanova's heads and led them to where we stood leaning against the hood of the pickup truck. "Thought I was here to do some menial labor," I said.

"Your dad thought you'd like to get a ride in, too. Levi and Silas are working on strong-willed calves who want their mommas to carry them, if they could." He looked over to Tristan.

Tristan tossed me the radio from the front seat, and I hooked it on the back of my belt. He held up the jacket he'd brought for me. "No thanks. I'm good," I said.

"No wild stuff, and you get to ride with me," Matt said. "Banshee's loving it out here." He patted her neck. "Sweet soul. She reminds me of a medieval novel, eerie yet enchanting."

"Thanks for coming back to get me, Chloe. I won't be asking for brownie points like Silas." Tristan mounted his ride. The saddle creaked as he threw his right leg over Casanova's hindquarters.

He set the stirrups and settled in. "Thanks for the ride, Matt." With one swift nudge and click of his tongue, he rode away.

I kicked at the damp ground.

"What was that about?" Matt asked.

The flecks of gold in his irises glimmered in the sunlight. "That guy has had a rough life," I said. "How come no one told me?"

Matt shrugged. "Maybe nobody thought they should be airing his business."

My belly stirred. "Kind of makes me think about things in a different light." I stroked Gypsy's mane.

"He's not so bad," Matt said, lowering his voice. "He's a great wrangler. He can ride circles around Levi and Silas."

Matt leaned closer until the brims of our hats touched. I scrunched up my nose at him. "Do I *really* have to ride with you?"

"Yep. Take it up with your dad if you don't like it. We're riding in pairs, and I drew the short straw," he answered.

"Lucky you," I said with a grin. "Maggie's taking Glad shopping today. Yesterday, she bought an antique wooden rocking horse for the baby." I gripped the saddle horn and stepped into Matt's cupped hands to mount Gypsy. I'd choose my stride with caution today. "Have you thought about my dad's offer?"

"Sure have. Been kind of waiting for a time to talk about it with you. Guess there's no perfect timing in a situation like this. I know how much you want to be co-CEO, and I don't want to come between you and your dad. That wouldn't be right." Matt mounted Trigger and settled into his saddle with ease.

"How much do you want it?" He didn't have to say anything; I could read the answer in his eyes. "I've been pushing buttons lately for a reason. The job means the world to me. I wouldn't have suggested it to Dad if it didn't."

"I don't want to butt heads with you over this. Position or no position, I'm not going anywhere. My investment here involves more than ranching and wrangling. It's clear your presence and opinion will always be valued. I suspect Ida May wasn't your granddaddy's official co-CEO, and from what I hear, she did more than love her man."

"I appreciate your consideration. And you're right about Ida May." The scent of wildflowers and leather washed over me like a warm blanket. When the breeze picked up, a woman's voice spoke to me. *He's the one.* "She was a smart woman." I imagined her riding alongside my dad toward the horizon. "Matt—"

"Yeah, Chloe?"

I couldn't finish my thought. Dad's offer to Matt left me feeling raw. I tugged my hat tight to my brow.

"Chloe—"

"Yeah, Matt?"

"Let's take it one day at a time. And right now, we have some riding to do." He paused. "You know, your dad and I just want you to be safe. And not just because you're pregnant." The dimple in his left cheek was as deep as the Grand Canyon.

I combed Gypsy's mane with my fingers, the twitch beneath my fingertips a sure sign she was ready to work.

Matt pulled Banshee's reins to the right and circled wide like a cattle dog securing the herd, his instincts just as loyal.

The corner of my mouth lifted. "Let's go find us some strays." I eased Gypsy into a trot. Her hips swayed to a lazy beat, and I settled in.

Matt rode alongside.

The crisp air cleared my head. I understood why Tristan wasn't like his brother. Justin's life seemed gentler. Tristan bore invisible scars, the worst kind—the kind that cut the deepest and took the most time to heal, if they could ever heal at all.

"I can't imagine losing you, Chloe. I don't know how Tristan gets up every day."

The hair bristled on my nape. "I'm sorry if I take you for granted," I said.

"I'm not sure where this baby will take us. But it'll certainly be interesting."

"I'm scared," I said.

"I know you are."

I sunk into my saddle. "Aren't you even a little scared?"

"I suspect there are plenty of guys out there who would be afraid, but I'm not. When you first told me, I was shocked, really shocked. After thinking and worrying about it, so much I couldn't sleep, I decided what was meant to be was meant to be." Matt rested his hand on his thigh. "Thought maybe if I simmered down, you might, too."

"How do you reckon that?" I asked.

He relaxed his shoulders. "I was out here one day, and my mind kept circling the idea of a baby like a high-strung cattle dog. Then this strange feeling washed through me like the morning river. I remember exactly where I was, what the sky looked like, and how each blade of grass, what's left of it, swayed in the breeze as I settled into my saddle, feeling okay."

"Where were you?"

Matt pointed across the field. "Over there by the stream. Near the ole willow."

I knew the spot well. "Grandpa and I used to come out here when I was a teenager. We'd ride along the stream and sit under that lone tree and have lunch when I was driving my dad crazy." I pictured us there now, in a hazy daydream. "Imagine that."

"Not hard to imagine at all. I'm surprised your dad is still standing."

"Hey," I said. "I bet you had your moments, too."

Matt's dimple returned. "I suppose I did, but my dad was pretty tough, not someone to be tested. His expectations of working hard in school—heck, working hard, period—and following rules were crystal clear. My older brother did all the hell-raising. My shenanigans were nothing compared to his."

"I can see that. Kibby likes his liquor. Do you think he'll get his act together and sober up?"

Matt shrugged. "Only time will tell. I hope so."

Gypsy craned her neck. She dipped her head, eyed the stream, and pulled the reins loose from my grip before nibbling on a tuft of grass she yanked from the ground.

"Come on," Matt said. "Everyone appears to be holding their own. Besides, we've got Tristan keeping an eye on pretty much everything and everyone."

"You're right about that."

"Seriously, you shouldn't give him such a hard time," Matt said.

"Dad and I will make a decision about who stays by morning."

"Tristan is all cowboy." Matt grinned. "He's got the moves. He's tough when he needs to be and understands the cattle and horses."

"And his instincts are spot-on," I said, taking in the lush valley view.

Matt perked up.

"Enough about business." I clicked my tongue at Gypsy to move along. She ducked her head beneath the branches of the willow canopy, the green foliage edged with a yellowish tinge. Banshee and Matt followed us.

Matt dismounted and tied Banshee to a hitching post my grandpa had sunk so the horses could wade and drink from the stream. I swung my leg over the back of Gypsy, and Matt held my waist as I rested my belly against the side of the saddle and slid down, feeling for the earth with the tips of my boots.

Matt turned me around and pushed his cowboy hat back from his forehead. His brow marked with a faint red line where the hat sat for hours on end. He lifted my chin with his finger, his leather glove cool against my skin.

More than Grandpa's spirit lingered. Ida May tickled my soul in unspoken ways, and I was paying attention. My granddad had been the hands-on teacher. More convinced than ever, I believed my grandmother had been working her magic all along even if I didn't recognize it until now.

"Being scared doesn't make you weak," Matt said.

I blinked away the emotion spreading like wildfire through my blood. Matt's faint smile fed the sensitivity I tried to push down deep inside me.

"You can't fool me, Chloe McIntyre. You're all about keeping up with the men around here."

He was right. I walked toward the stream. This time, I searched for Ida May's image in my reflection.

Matt tied Gypsy next to Banshee. His footsteps rustled in the tall grass behind me. The branches of the old tree reached over the stream and to the other bank. A boulder sat smack dab in the middle of the shallow water. "Grandpa used to hoist me up on that rock. I'd sit there and listen while he told me his cowboy stories."

"I bet he had some great ones," Matt said.

"He did." I wiggled my fingers to loosen time's grip. Coming unglued in front of Matt wasn't on this day's or any day's agenda. I stood at the edge of the water and listened. Matt stood beside me, and I held his hand.

"Matt, what's the thing you fear most?"

"Regret," he said, his gaze fixed on the horizon.

CHAPTER 18

TRISTAN KEPT HIS distance and spent the day working close to Quinn, which meant running errands and working behind the scenes to tie up loose ends. I suspected he needed his space after opening up about his family. I suspected he knew I needed my space, too.

I took my saddle to the barn and hung the bridle on its respective hook. Not only did I carve my name into the wood, two years later, I'd carved Gypsy's name below it with the jackknife Dad gave me for my fourteenth birthday. The thought to ask for a shiny silver nameplate hadn't occurred to me until later, and now thinking back, the rough, jagged letters dug into the timber suited me fine.

Silas sauntered in with Samson in his arms. The lazy dog's half-masted eyelids and his paws twitched like they did when he slept hard.

"Where did you disappear today after corralling the horses? I turned around and you were gone."

"Your dad asked me to look at your granddaddy's old truck. The engine was knocking. Working in my old man's gas station comes in handy now and then. We're gonna try some better fuel, and I changed the spark plugs. So far, so good."

Coal ran through my legs and over Silas's boots. Samson lifted his head and rested it against Silas's chest.

"You and Matt seem to have a good thing here." His smile disappeared beneath his beard.

"How long ago did you break up?" I picked Coal up and scratched her ears.

"Three months and eight days," he answered.

"This is where I'd say something clever if I thought I could help. I'm not exactly a relationship guru." I set Coal down, leaned against the stall door, and crossed my arms. Silas's sadness tugged at my heart. He was indeed a gentle giant.

"I figured." He rubbed Samson's belly, then set him down on a bale of hay. "There's nothing wrong with showing affection."

I grimaced. "This conversation just turned an uncomfortable corner."

"What's weird about that? It's life. We're adults," he said. "I suspect if I work for you and your daddy, we'll have personal conversations."

I wasn't so sure. "Well, you don't need to worry about too many of those. I like to stick to business.”

“Sometimes business *is* people.” He pushed his hat back from his forehead.

“You’re right. You ready for the smoked brisket tomorrow night? I can’t wait.” The bitter memory of barbeque tainted my thoughts. “I love a tender beef sandwich and a good Montana brewed beer. Gosh, being pregnant is taxing.”

“See, you can talk personal, but I have to say talking about pregnancy gets me a little squeamish.”

I laughed. “You’re rich. Gets me a little squeamish, too, but I’m trying my best to deal with it.”

“Is it harder than tending to animals, organizing wranglers, and digging ditches?”

“For me, yes. A whole ’nother mindset.”

Silas chuckled. “We should probably get back to work.”

“I haven’t eaten all afternoon. Wanna take a quick break and raid the refrigerator? I won’t tell the boss.”

“Sure, I’m always hungry.” Silas opened his arms, and Coal jumped up. Her paws landed with a soft thud against his chest. “This barn sure is tidy. Some places I’ve worked, not so organized.”

“There’s no slacking off around here, especially

if you're the owner's daughter." I thought I saw a few snowflakes today." I paused. "I'm not ready for colder weather."

We made our way to the main house.

"Did you know that no two snowflakes are alike and that they have six sides like a hexagon?" He held the mudroom door open.

"Well, you're full of surprises. Bet you didn't learn that at your daddy's gas station."

"Nope."

"Silas." My gaze met his.

"Yes, Ms. McIntyre."

I liked how my name rolled from his tongue. Ms. McIntyre was formal yet fitting. "If we choose another candidate for the job opening, where will you go?"

"I got my feelers out there. I'm resourceful and usually land on my feet."

I scuffed my boots against the bristly doormat, took off my hat, and set it on the counter next to a note Maggie wrote. "She and Glad drove into Livingston." I checked the clock on the stove. "They should be home soon. Wonder what's for dinner tonight."

I opened the fridge door and inspected the contents. I pulled out the loaf of bread and the huckleberry jam. "I'm having peanut butter and jelly. Can you see if there are any chips in the cupboard behind you?"

"Sure." Silas pulled out two bags. "Which one do you want?"

I hemmed and hawed. He put both bags on the island. "Good choice. I'll have both. On second thought, give me the plain ones and put the barbeque chips away." A sour note pinched my stomach. "I won't be eating those for a long, long time. Want a sandwich?"

"Yes, ma'am." Silas guzzled the glass of ice water he'd poured for himself. "Want some?"

"Please." He slid a full glass in front of me. I drained it and asked for more. Silas filled it up while I slathered whole wheat bread with peanut butter and preserves.

"You're quite the sandwich maker. That'll come in handy. Kids love PB&J." Silas opened multiple cupboards, searching for plates until he found them. "This probably isn't any of my business, but where will you live when the baby comes?"

I stopped eating, put my sandwich down, and sat on a stool at the counter. I hadn't thought about it. I assumed I'd stay on with Dad and Maggie, but how would Matt fit into the equation? Would Matt even *want* to fit into the equation?

We hadn't discussed it.

Silas bit off almost half of his sandwich. His jaw muscles flexed as he chewed, and his gaze inspected me. I cut the crust from my bread and put it on the side of my plate. Silas questioned the waste. "I'm not a crust girl. I like the guts. I call dibs on the centerpiece of anything that bakes in a pan." Jam oozed onto my hand when I bit into my sandwich. Silas stuffed his mouth with chips and continued to watch me.

"What?" I said with a mouthful of food.

"Nothing," he mumbled. He swallowed then drained his glass of water. He went to the fridge and pulled out the lemonade.

"Have a beer for me. It's almost five. These nine months just got longer and more stressful."

He popped the top on the frosty can of Montana brewed beer. "Want to smell it?" He held it in my direction.

"It's not the same," I replied.

Silas's laugh was followed by the sound of Dad stomping off his boots in the mudroom.

"We're in here, Dad," I said. "Want a sandwich?"

"Sure." He tossed his hat on the counter and greeted Silas with a pat on the back.

I liked his bald dome. The cropped salt-and-pepper hairs on the sides of his head matched the scruff on his face. Dad rubbed his stubbly chin like he always did after coming in from outside. I made him a sandwich and put it on my plate. He ate my leftover crusts before taking a bite. I smiled at Silas. "We've got a system here."

Silas checked his phone and excused himself.

"You and Tristan did a nice job working together out there. Levi's feeding the horses," Dad said, reaching for the bag of chips.

My gaze held his. "No problem."

"Tristan's had a rough go of it."

"How come nobody told me he lost his wife and son?"

Dad leaned against the back of the stool. Thinking lines mapped his forehead, and he massaged them away. "Didn't think it was my place to go talking about his business."

"That's what Matt said. But you could've given me a head's up. Losing his wife and son in a car accident is horrific. I would've cut him some slack."

"Maybe I should have told you." Dad cleared his throat. "Chloe, losing loved ones tragically is something you never recover from."

"I can't even imagine. I feel bad."

"Maybe you shouldn't feel bad for him—just

treat him like you treat anybody else around here. With respect and kindness. When you're talking to him, pretend you're talking to *yourself*," Dad said.

I pulled the bandana from my head. "That's the thing, Dad. I'm not always easy on myself."

"You'll learn."

Silas poked his head into the kitchen. "Is it okay if I join you again, sir?"

Dad gestured for Silas to come in.

"Do you mind if I have another beer? I wouldn't normally ask, but the first one went down so easily. And I think I'm done for the day."

Dad nodded.

Silas opened the fridge door and got another cold one. He popped the top and took a long draw.

"You're having another beer in front of the woman who can't have one?"

"He's our guest, and besides, he got my father's truck working again," Dad said.

"Can't argue with that," I said.

"Wise move." Dad ate the last of his sandwich. "Where's Maggie?" he asked with a mouthful.

"She'll be home soon." I pushed her note toward Dad and watched him read it.

He pointed to Silas. "You want to get me one of those beers, son?"

Silas opened the refrigerator door. "There ya' go, sir." He slid it across the counter.

Amusement appeared at the corners of Dad's eyes. "You'd make an excellent bartender. Not only can you talk to the animals, you're quick and have a smooth delivery."

Silas tapped his can against Dad's. "Cheers," he said.

"You two ready for the cowboy dinner tomorrow? It's gonna be a big day. Glad is riding Huckleberry," Dad said.

I gulped down the rest of my cold water. "Refreshing," I declared. "I can't wait."

Dad drained his beer, stood, and gestured for his hat. Silas tossed it to him. Dad kissed the crown of my head. "We have some things to discuss later. Pencil me in," he said.

"Like what?" I asked.

"We'll talk later." He rested his hand on my shoulder. "I'm going outside to finish up with the boys."

"It's funny how you call them *boys*." I studied Silas, who was all man.

"They're like sons to me. Fine young men," he said.

I wondered if he knew I'd spent my life trying to be the son he never had.

TRISTAN AVOIDED ME for the rest of the day. After missing dinner, Justin packed him some leftovers and took them to the bunkhouse after dessert. Levi and Silas passed on the bonfire invite.

"Chloe, do you have a minute?" Dad gestured for me to follow him into his office. He poured himself a cocktail and settled into his favorite leather chair.

I perused the brochures on Dad's desk. "You're looking at new trucks?"

He nodded, then sipped his bourbon. "Just shopping at this point." He propped his feet up on the ottoman. "We should talk about our three fine candidates."

I settled in the leather chair across from him. "Sure. What are you thinking?"

"You know what I'm thinking. I'd like Tristan to join us. But I know you two have your differences."

I kicked off my boots and tucked my feet beneath me. "I still wish I would've known about his family."

Dad peered over the rim of his glass. "I was hoping you two would get along. You're both strong-willed, stubborn, and have a head for animals."

I rested my head against the back of the chair.

"I haven't been very nice to him, have I?" I put up my hand, the flutter in my belly a very real reminder of how my life was changing. "Don't answer. I know I haven't. I want to be the best here. I've got a lot to prove. I don't want anyone outdoing me or taking my place." I tucked my hair behind my ears. "Not Tristan, not Silas, not even Levi. And before you say anything, Silas and Levi are easier to be nice to because I know they're not staying on."

"That's what you're worried about?"

"Yes. I admit it."

He swirled the last of the amber-colored liquor in his glass. "No one could ever take your place. Not Tristan, not Silas, not Levi, *not Matt*. I was straight with you about bringing him on as co-CEO. You're gonna have your hands full. He's qualified, and he's got something more here than just a job now." He finished his drink. "Bringing a baby into this world doesn't make you any less of a rancher. I know I don't talk about Ida May, but maybe it's time I do. She toted me around from the day I was born to the day I could walk and sit in the saddle with her. She taught me to ride and buck up when I struggled. Some days when I lose my footing, I swear I can feel her arms around me. And boy, could she ride and rope. Slowing down wasn't in her vocabulary any more than it's in yours. Her presence rivaled my daddy's and then some."

"What would she think of me?"

Dad threw back his head with a hearty laugh. "She'd think you were the cat's meow. She'd tell me I was soft on you growing up." He rubbed his chin. "She'd want you to follow in her footsteps."

I pushed my shoulders back. "I bet she always spoke her piece." Dad stood and offered me his hand. I gladly took it.

"You know she did, and when she sold someone short, she apologized." He paused. "What do you say we go relax by the fire? Your granddaddy's guitar is calling me."

"Sure. Would it be okay if we beefed up Levi's and Silas's wages for their time?"

"Already planned on it. I have to say, the past few days have been mighty interesting. Having them around surely validated Tristan's worth."

"Agreed. We'll talk to him in the morning about joining us full-time." I slipped into my cowboy boots. "These old things are like butter on my feet."

"You need new boots, kid."

"Doesn't seem right leaving this pair behind, just yet."

Dad wrapped his arm around my shoulders, and we headed outside.

JUSTIN STEPPED FROM the shadows and sat next to me. His usual smile was turned upside down.

"What's with the long face?"

He nudged his hat back and rubbed his jaw. "I probably shouldn't bring this up in front of everyone. I was hoping to catch you alone."

"We're family, son. If you've got something to say, we're here for you." Dad set his guitar down.

The scorn in Justin's stare obliterated the contented feeling I'd finally achieved after the long day. The hair on my nape stood at attention.

"Tristan packed up his horses and left. There, I said it." Anger flashed in his words. "As much as I wanted this to work out, guess you won out in the end, bosslady."

I pushed my shoulders back and didn't say anything. As I glanced around the firepit, brooding gazes were upon me.

Being pregnant seemed like the least of my worries.

CHAPTER 19

WITHOUT TRISTAN AMONG us, the tone of the morning was off. I kept my head down while rounding up the horses from the mountain. Silas rode alongside, whistling a somber tune. His attention focused on the stragglers.

Levi hadn't come prepared for the chilly morning temperature and borrowed a shearling lined jacket from Dad. Quinn had stayed close to Levi, reminding him of the routine. By the time we rode in, Levi sounded like one of the guys.

After the horses were corralled, Quinn pulled me aside as the wranglers headed in for breakfast. He was the quiet one in the brood. He didn't question protocol, did what was expected, and went out of his way to run errands for Dad. His dark stare met mine.

"You know I'm not one to debate the decisions you and your father make. It's not my place, but I have something to say." He slapped his gloves against his chaps. "I know I don't get a say in who you hire, but I think you've made a mistake."

I propped my foot on the bottom rail of the fence. "I'm sorry you feel that way. Tristan chose to bow out." By the expression on Quinn's face, he wasn't buying what I was selling.

"Chloe, you've got tremendous pull. You've got determination, and you ain't afraid to stand your ground. I respect that."

"I feel a *but* coming on here." I bowed my head.

"And mighty smart." He tucked his gloves in his back pocket. "We all know Levi isn't what this ranch needs. Silas has a way with the animals, and I'm sure he could hold his own in any situation, but..."

"But what? This conversation stays between us."

"But you know when you're picking teams in gym class?"

I nodded. The sinking feeling in my stomach wasn't morning sickness.

"Tristan would've been my first pick. That's all."

"Why?" I held his gaze.

"Because he's the one I'd want to have my back if there was trouble. He's not afraid to take initiative. He's got a way with animals, and when we disagree, he respects the difference. Kind of like the person standing next to me." He paused. "Not to mention, there's something to be said for common sense."

I nodded and walked away.

"Chloe—"

I turned on a heel. "Yeah, Quinn?"

"Are we still good?"

"We're good. I'll meet you inside for breakfast."

Matt's silhouette appeared at the end of the drive, Trigger's swagger one of confidence. Matt sat tall with the sun on his shoulders, his cowboy hat low across his brow. He dismounted, and I shaded my eyes to see him better.

He led Trigger to the hitching post and wrapped the reins around the weathered wood. Trigger pawed at the ground with a snort.

"I guess he'd rather be in the field with the cattle," I said.

"He would." Matt took off his gloves and stuffed them in his back pocket. He noticed Quinn shuffling into the barn. "Everything okay?"

"Fine."

Dad joined us, his forehead knit tight.

"Well, we've got some chatting to do. Thought maybe we could have a few minutes before breakfast," he said.

I tucked my fingers in the back pockets of my jeans. "Sure."

"Wasn't quite the same without Tristan this morning," Dad said. "His absence put a different light on Silas and Levi. Silas seemed a bit skittish without his competition. Almost like following Tristan's lead gave him focus." Dad crossed his arms over his chest.

"I agree," Matt said.

Dad and Matt looked at me. I couldn't disagree. I'd laid awake last night thinking about Tristan's exit. "I never dreamed he'd pack up and leave," I said.

Justin appeared from the barn shadows. His heavy shuffle mimicked his long face. "Sorry. I didn't mean to eavesdrop. I stayed behind to make sure the water spigot was off."

I tugged at the brim of my hat, avoiding his stare. The water spigot hadn't been on. His comment wasn't the usual rib I was used to. Matt leaned against the fence and pushed his hat back from his forehead.

"I think I can speak for all of us. Tristan was missed this morning," Dad said.

Justin held my stare. "Mostly by me. He didn't want to stay if it was going to be a problem. He's got enough on his plate." He paused. "I've worked here for a long time. I was looking forward to working the land and the animals with family."

Dad kicked at the dirt. Matt stood quietly, and I stepped closer to Justin. "You gonna leave, too?" I ignored the flash of anger in his eyes. "I know you well enough to think you're contemplating it. I see it in your face."

"Yep. Anyone who doesn't want my brother probably doesn't want me," Justin said.

His words stung. I couldn't imagine not having Justin around. I suspected Dad had something to say, but this was my doing, and we both knew it was up to me to fix it. "If there's anyone I want to stay on, it's you. You're more than a hired hand, especially to me."

"Tristan rode circles around Levi and Silas. Tristan's the best wrangler I know, and I'm not saying that because he's my brother. I wouldn't have brought him here if I didn't think he'd be a good fit. And he would've been a *great* fit." Justin rubbed his chin. "This would've been the perfect place for him to find his footing again."

Matt stepped forward, and Justin gestured for him to stand down. "I don't mean any disrespect. This is between Chloe and me." Justin stood taller and lifted his chin. "Did you mean what you said about me being more than a hired hand?"

"Yes," I answered. If Dad's stone-faced expression was an indication, I was on my own. There wasn't time to debate or doubt myself.

"Tristan's interest isn't to out-do anyone or prove his purpose. He came here because he's at a crossroads. No different than Levi, who belongs in a vineyard, or Silas, who's escaping a broken heart. Who, by the way, sits outside the bunkhouse playing his harmonica before lights out, but you wouldn't know any of this because you've got your head somewhere else. We all have something in common, and I would've thought you of all people would've recognized—"

I touched his arm. "I need to interrupt."

Justin stood quietly, then said, "Dang, Chloe. He's broken. You of all people should understand." He let out a long breath.

"I screwed up. Tristan may not have had something to prove, but I did." I filled my lungs with crisp morning air. Hopefully, Justin would hear me out. "Where can I reach him?"

"When he's done, he's done. He's like that. No looking back." Justin took off his gloves. His gaze met Dad's then Matt's.

"Maybe so, but I'm not done. I want you to stay. I'm sure Dad, Matt, and the rest do too."

"I'm gonna need some time. Maybe now's the

time to head back to school for good," he replied.

I looked at Dad.

"Why don't you take the day to think, son? We've got enough hands to help out." Dad held Justin's stare. "You're welcome to join us for breakfast. If you'd rather not, I understand. I bet Chloe wouldn't mind fixing you a plate and delivering it to the bunkhouse."

"I appreciate the accommodations, sir. I think it might be best." He turned on a heel, walked through the barn and out the other end toward the bunkhouse.

Dad knocked his hat back from his forehead. "Chloe."

My name sounded rough rolling from his tongue. I mumbled a few choice words under my breath before Dad took me by the arm. Matt buried his head in his hands.

"I'll get Justin's meal. By the time I get to the bunkhouse, he'll have settled down." By the expression on my father's face, he wasn't buying what I was selling either.

"For all our sakes, I hope you're right," Dad said.

The three of us walked back to the house in silence. Instead of making my oatmeal, I fixed Justin a plate of red velvet pancakes and elk sausage, then got into Grandpa's truck to deliver it to him. Just as I turned the key, Justin drove past in his jeep, down the drive toward the main road. I shifted the engine into drive and hit the gas. The engine sputtered twice then died. I pushed the door open and hopped out.

Quinn called from the porch as he started Maggie's SUV with the key fob. "Did you break your granddaddy's truck already?"

I skipped up the steps and grabbed the fob from him. "Sorry, cowboy. This is an emergency."

"Hey! Come back here."

I grabbed Justin's breakfast, jumped into the SUV, and buckled up. "I gotta go. Did Justin say where he was headed?"

"How would I know? What am I gonna tell your daddy?"

I shrugged. "Don't know, but I gotta go. I can't lose Justin." I put the vehicle into gear, sped down the drive and over the bridge, leaving a trail of dust behind me. I kept my distance behind Justin and called Dad.

"Hey, Chloe. Quinn says you snatched the keys and took off."

"I did. Justin drove off without his breakfast, and he's not going to leave us too. Not sure when I'll be back. And by the way, Grandpa's truck died."

"I know. You sure chasing the boy is a good idea?"

"I don't know, but I'm gonna find out. What if he doesn't come back?"

Dad sighed into the phone. "Call me if you need me."

"Sure. Bye."

The gorge shone bright in the morning sun. I rolled down the window. The breeze washed over me, and I couldn't remember the last time I'd had a day off.

About ten miles down the road, Justin veered onto a hidden drive leading to his favorite fishing spot near the bend in the river. I pulled over and waited on the gravel shoulder until I was sure he wasn't turning around. I'd give him plenty of time to get settled before making my next move.

I drove down the narrow road, wondering what I'd say to him or if he'd even talk to me. I parked behind him. I grabbed the canister of bear spray from underneath the seat, got out of the truck, grabbed Justin's breakfast, and quietly shut the door. I leaned against the bumper, soaking up the sun. I'd been fishing with Justin plenty of times to know how long it took him to get to the boulder and set his gear.

Tying flies and practicing casting back at the

ranch was mere practice for days spent on the river. The last time we'd gone fishing, we'd bet a six-pack of beer and an elk tenderloin on the daily catch. Justin had caught three more trout than me, and I never heard the end of it.

I walked down the trail leading to the place he deemed *his spot*. The purple lupine near the riverbank had gone to seed and turned browned. The last of the shooting stars bowed their heads. Justin stood in the middle of the river. He flicked his wrist and released the fishing line. The sound of the cast was like music to my ears. I found a seat and waited for him to notice me. Leaning back on my elbows, I tipped my chin to the sky.

"You're gonna sit there a long time before I talk to you," he said.

I picked a daisy and sniffed it. "I can wait."

"How'd you find me?"

"That wasn't much of a wait." I picked up a thin flat skipping rock and inspected it before setting it down. Scaring away the fish would give him another reason to storm off. "I saw you leave. Probably would've been better to leave after Dad and I rode out for the morning. Besides, you left without breakfast." I showed him the container of food.

Justin tugged on his line while eying the shadows floating beneath the water's surface. "Guess I should've thought my hasty exit through. Shouldn't you be back at the ranch working?"

"I *am* working," I said.

He reeled in his line and made his way over to where I sat.

"You're not gonna leave, are you?"

"Did you get new waders?"

The vein in his neck bulged. "Yes. And your dad said I could have the day to think."

"He did, but I'm not him. It wasn't his idea to follow you. And we can't have a wrangler thinking on an empty stomach. Red velvet pancakes and elk sausage."

"He would never chase me down, but you possess an unusual arsenal of tactics when it comes to getting what you want."

I crossed my legs and sat like a pretzel, wishing I had a whole bag of pretzels. My belly growled. "I'm really sorry. I was a jerk to Tristan. Last night, Dad and I talked. We were going to tell him the job was his." I kicked at the ground, mustering up the courage I needed to make the situation right. "You were right. Tristan's top billing. Truth is, I was jealous he was so good." I paused. "And so you know, I've never chased a guy down before. Never wanted to until I saw you drive away this morning.”

Justin sighed. “You’re impossible.”

“I know. And usually impossible to stay upset with. Will you please not quit? We can’t lose you too,” I said.

“Your daddy told me I had the day to think.”

“Yes, he did. And now so will I. I hope you catch scads of fish and enjoy your time alone. I’m sorry.” I stood and turned to leave.

“Chloe—”

“Yeah, Justin.” I glanced back at him.

“Why should I stay?”

“Because you want to. Because you’re family.” I tugged at the brim of my hat and held his gaze. “Where can I find Tristan?”

“Wish I knew.”

CHAPTER 20

MAGGIE KNOCKED ON the doorjamb. I slid on my worn cowboy boots. "Dad thinks I need new ones. I must if he thinks so. Almost have a hole clean through near the toe." I pulled my faded jeans over the top of the supple leather, then tucked the boots my mother had sent beneath the bed.

"Good morning to you, too. You should've gone with us yesterday. Glad bought boots."

"Probably should have. Maybe Tristan wouldn't have left." I smoothed down my pants and shook out my legs. "Did you get new boots?"

She lifted her dark denim pant leg and showed off the teal-colored shaft of her new boots. "A present to myself for finishing my book project. I couldn't resist the indigo birds and flowers. Didn't even notice the tiny hearts until Mom pointed them out."

Maggie inspected my room decorated with horse photos, riding trophies, and old college mementos. "I know it's a little outdated," I said.

"It's about time for a serious makeover," she replied. "We'll chat later. I heard you rummaging around in here, so I thought I'd pop in." She eyed the pile of jeans in the corner.

"I had a wardrobe malfunction." I held up the jeans with the tear in the seat. "Can't wear these anymore. Thought I'd hit the secondhand store." I folded the ripped jeans and set them on the bed.

"I bet we could find you some cute jeans at a maternity store," she said cautiously. "We could order online and skip shopping altogether. You could keep what works and send back what doesn't." Dimples framed her mouth. "Trust me, a stretchy waistband will change your life."

"You've already shopped for me, haven't you?"

"I know how much you don't like it, and, well, I couldn't help myself. Nothing good ever comes from pouring yourself into a tight pair of jeans. I'll send it all back if you want me to," she answered.

"Not necessary. I'd love to look at what you ordered. I didn't realize how fast I'd grow out of my clothes. Thank you." I reached for her hand. "Are you coming out to the barn?"

"Not sure yet. Glad wants to see what I'm working on. I've set up a table in the room at the end of the hall. It's slowly becoming a workspace-slash-office for me. I found an antique oak desk yesterday in Livingston. I'm gonna need some wranglers to help me get it up the stairs."

"Well, we know where to find those." I flashed a toothy smile. "I can't wait to see what you're doing in there. I'll check it out later, after I get cleaned up." We left my bedroom together. She went one way, and I went the other.

I thought about Maggie making the empty room into her office. Guess the room where no one ever went wouldn't be an option for a baby's room.

Samson laid on the mat by the back door. "You can come with me, boy." He sat up and yawned. Judging from his pout, I had interrupted the best nap ever. I slipped on a flannel jacket, and the two of us made our way to the barn.

After grooming Huckleberry, I put one of Grandpa's favorite saddles on her. Huckleberry and Glad deserved the best. I tightened the girth, then patted Huck's neck. "You take good care of Gladiola today. We want her in one piece." Huckleberry batted her lashes. I dug in my pocket and fed her some sugar. Her soft nose tickled my skin. "I love you, girl." She let out a muffled whinny and held my stare. "You'll always be my girl," I told her. "You were my first horse, my teacher, my heart."

"Too bad these animals don't get any attention around here."

I smiled at Matt, who leaned against the wooden support column. His arms crossed over his chest. "How long have you been standing there?"

"Long enough to hear your sweet talk," he said.

"Don't tell anyone." I ran my hand across Huckleberry's thick hindquarter. "Soft as ever." Her tail brushed my hand.

"They already know. Ain't no secret how much you love these animals." Matt pulled me close. "You're mighty pretty, Chloe McIntyre."

"Stop it," I said as my belly touched his. "Someone will see us."

"So?" he mumbled.

The speculation of challenge resonated in Matt's response. His hands were on my waist, his thumbs hooked through my belt loops.

"You really should have a warmer jacket on," he said.

"This is a jacket." I raised an eyebrow at him. "What's gotten into you?"

"You have. There's something different about you today. I saw it at the breakfast table."

Matt held me close. Heat from his touch warmed me through. I tugged at the collar of my flannel shirt.

"What's the matter?"

My cheeks smoldered. I swallowed hard and held his stare. The golden flecks in his dark eyes were doing more than holding my attention. I flicked the brim of his hat. "Why do you have to be so darn handsome?"

Matt's wide smile beckoned the dimple in his left cheek. "Now we're talking," he said.

"Is that so, cowboy?"

I leaned back in his arms. Matt pushed the hair away from my cheeks and tucked it behind my ears. He fingered the bandana on my head.

"I want it to be like this forever. Just my best friend, me, and my favorite pony." Huckleberry's nudge an affirmation that I wasn't asking too much.

"Don't let Gypsy hear you say that. She can be temperamental, like someone else I know."

"Is that right?" I ran my fingers across Matt's jawline, down his neck then through his thick hair. A baby would change moments like this.

"Now, what's the matter?" Matt asked, holding my face.

"Nothing. I'm seeing a man and a young girl walk across the cattle field, but I can't make out faces. I'm not sure if it's you or not."

"Most likely your granddad."

My breath caught in my chest. Goose bumps covered my body, and Grandpa's image flashed in my mind.

"Winston sure did have a magic touch with this place. Hope my luck raising cattle is half of what he had. You know, when he's not riding alongside, he's up on the ridge taking in the view." Matt blinked away the furrow in his brow.

Listening to him talk about Grandpa grabbed my heart like he was roping a stray and jerking it a little bit closer to him. "And Ida May's right by his side."

"Chloe, maybe you were supposed to get pregnant." He paused. "Maybe it was His plan. Maybe their plan."

The hair stood up on my nape. A knot grew at the back of my throat.

"I'm sorry, Chloe. I didn't mean to upset you." Matt pulled a bandana from his back pocket. "I don't think things are always meant to be easy."

Matt's fingertips brushed my cheek. I nuzzled into the palm of his hand like Huckleberry when she looked for sugar.

"Chloe, what's the girl look like?"

"She's wearing a loose, white sundress. Her long, brown braids are tied with ribbons. Why?"

My gaze searched his. Matt slipped his hand under my shirt and rested it on my belly. My stomach fluttered at his touch.

"Are your granddad and the girl walking toward you or away?" he asked, hesitantly.

I closed my eyes. A sunny haze filled my mind. The girl skipped through the green field dotted with yellow wildflowers. A thin smile tickled my lips. The image grew stronger. My heart thumped wildly. Winston was bringing her home. Ida May stood in the background, shooing them toward me.

I didn't want the vision to end.

Please don't leave me, I pleaded to the flickering images in my head. I bit my bottom lip. "I want them to stay with me. I need them to stay." My words drifted away like a message in a bottle lost in the ocean tide.

Grandpa, Ida May, and the girl disappeared. Matt's lips grazed my forehead like the kiss of sunshine on a chilly Montana morning. I rested my head on his chest, his heartbeat strong. He rested his chin on top of my head.

Stay with me.

I fingered his flannel jacket. "Will you help me saddle up Cora? Maggie's running late."

"Sure thing," Matt replied.

The corner of my lips curled toward the barn

rafters. Matt kissed my forehead and held my hands in his. The toes of our boots touched. "If I stood on your feet, would you dance with me?"

"Sure would, but I think you'd be happier dancing to your own tune," he said.

"You're probably right." I wasn't a girl anymore looking for someone else to lead the way. I was my own woman, and I wanted to be in control.

CHAPTER 21

I LEANED AGAINST the split rail fence. Maggie and Gladiola walked toward me. Each woman an individual, an identity, clearly defined lighting the way for the other and those they met along the way. A balance I desired to achieve.

The horses were saddled and ready to go. Glad's casual ride had turned into an afternoon event. Dad, Trout, Quinn, and Silas came in from the field to meet us. Matt put his arm around my shoulder, and we watched them ride in.

"Levi appreciated his bonus. Said he'd be back someday," Matt said.

"Hope he brings wine." I picked up a feather lying in the grass and stuck it in the band of Matt's hat. "Silas was pleased with the offer to stay on, but I'd feel better if I could track Tristan down."

"You've left messages. You've apologized to Justin."

"I guess it's time to move forward. A costly lesson learned," I admitted.

Maggie snapped photos of the men on their

horses as they strode past. The absence of Justin and Tristan pinched. Justin had rounded up the horses with us first thing, then drove off to do errands for Dad, his cool distance a reminder of the hurt I caused.

"Nothing better than a brood of wranglers riding together," Matt said.

"You should have been with them." I nudged him.

He tapped on his chest. "I was, in here," he said. "I had other business. But I'll tell you about that later."

The line of horses tied to the hitching post made for the perfect postcard.

"I hear you ladies need an escort," Dad said as Breeze sniffed Maggie's hair. She patted Breeze's neck.

"I'd take him up on it if I were you," Glad said.

She was decked out in denim, new cowboy booties, and one of Maggie's flannel jackets, the fleece collar downy as her gentle disposition. She reached for Maggie's hand, and they meandered toward the mounting block.

Glad climbed the two steps. Matt hopped up next to her while I maneuvered Huckleberry into position. "Huckleberry is as sweet as they come," I told her. "All you have to do is hold on. She'll do all the work, and if she doesn't, she knows there'll be no treats." Huckleberry poked me with her nose. She understood what I was saying.

Matt showed Glad how to put her foot in the stirrup, then helped her into the saddle.

"It's been a while, but I've got this," she said.

Dad helped Maggie mount Cora and checked the girth.

Justin drove up in his dusty jeep, and I watched him from the corner of my eye. Matt checked, then double-checked Glad's saddle. She declined the helmet Maggie offered her.

"I know how you feel," I said.

"You're not helping, Chloe." Maggie leaned on her saddle horn.

"Sorry." I ran my fingers through Gypsy's mane.

"We're not going far, girl. Just up the river and back." Gypsy swished her tail and whinnied. I stood in my stirrups, leaned forward, and gave her some sugar.

"I saw that," Dad said. "No wonder these horses do whatever you tell them."

Matt put his foot in the stirrup and hoisted himself up onto Butch. "I get the big boy today," he said.

Butch was three hands taller than Gypsy. He had thicker withers and stocky hindquarters. "Sure is a pretty tail. Glad to see you've stayed out of the burrs," I said, settling into one of the old working saddles.

Justin got out of the truck and greeted Matt. I held his stare, dismounted, and caught up to him as he went into the barn. "Hold up," I called.

"What, Chloe?"

"Please, come with us."

"It's not like you to beg." He hung the new tool belt on a nail.

"No, it's not. I'm not the only one who'd like you to join us. Trigger's bent out of shape because Matt's giving Butch a workout today." I paused. "I'm glad you decided to stay. Have you heard from Tristan?"

"I haven't." He tucked his thumbs in his pockets.

"Come with us." I squeezed his hand.

"Not today. I should stay here. Someone has to man the fort while you're out playing," he said.

"Is that what you think we're doing? Or did you just say that to be mean?" My temper resonated in my words.

"Let's not do this. They're waiting for you."

"Fine." I turned on a heel, then turned back around. "I'd do anything to get your brother back here."

"You sure about that?"

"I'm sure. Hope your chores suit you fine." I tugged at the brim of my hat.

Matt and I brought up the rear after everyone departed. I rode quietly, taking in the scenery of pines and the trees starting to turn fiery shades of orange, red, and yellow. I wished on the babbling creek to wash my disappointed feelings away.

Matt did a double-take. "Are you okay?"

I nodded. "Dad looks like Grandpa."

My dad rode tall, his shoulders pushed back, proud of his *boys*, and his family. Although Silas resembled Paul Bunyan compared to the rest of us.

"I told you before, and I'll say it again. Good ole Winston is everywhere." The corner of Matt's mouth lifted.

"And Ida May is right by his side."

When he was alive, Grandpa would tell me that my grandma spoke to him when he was wrangling and riding free. The outdoors was their connection. The outdoors was my connection too. I should've paid attention sooner. She was the breeze kissing my cheeks and the shiver down my spine. I kept an ear pressed to the sky, listening for her.

"This will be a nice ride. We're staying close to the river and taking it slow," Matt said in an easy voice, his strong, defined profile the mere outline of a hard-working wrangler with soul and integrity. "Just as it should be."

The image of the dark-haired girl returned. Her dark braids bobbed as she skipped along. Her features were delicate and clear, the forget-me-nots she carried vibrant and fresh. Her green eyes faded, and she disappeared. My breath caught in my chest.

Matt shifted his weight in his saddle. We veered onto the trail running parallel to the river. Soft sounds of babbling water lulled our carefree group of riders. The aroma of sage washed over us like a magic curtain.

Maggie broke stride, pulling her reins to the left and circling back around.

"You doing okay, Mom?" she asked.

"I want a horse," she replied.

"Of course you do. Not sure a pony will fit into your carry-on though." Maggie rested her hand on Cora's rump and turned to see me better. "You two doing okay back here?"

"Yup." I smiled.

"You gonna take our picture?" Matt asked.

"Great idea." Maggie lifted the camera hanging around her neck on a wide black strap. "I'll snap a few, and we'll see what happens."

"I'll skip the pony. I'd like a pretty roan like

your Cora." Glad peeked over her shoulder, showing off a giddy smile.

"You're a natural, Gladiola. Make sure those cowboys do their jobs. They're here to dote on you," I told her.

"This is the life," she replied.

"I didn't sell my house in Michigan all those years ago for nothing. This place can steal your heart if you're not careful, Mom."

"You keep on telling me that, Maggie Jean, and you might find me on your doorstep someday."

Cora fell in line behind Gypsy. We neared the weeping willow, and Dad slowed up. He inspected us with McIntyre pride as we gathered around him. He was going to be a grandpa, and he'd be the best of the best because he'd followed in his father's footsteps.

"You all ready to head back? We're about thirty out. Glad, how ya' doing?"

"Yeehaw," she called with a fist pump.

Dad circled us. He nodded to me, then to Matt. There was something new in the spark between them, an unspoken respect.

"Why don't you and Matt take the lead, and I'll bring up the rear with Maggie," Dad said.

Matt pulled his reins to the right. I circled in the opposite direction. Gypsy wanted to run, and so did I. The spring in her step equaled my natural intensity. There was something deep inside that revved and purred, coaxing me to listen. The urge to break free from the pack consumed me, but I pushed it down, hard as it was.

I fidgeted, unable to soak in the ease surrounding me.

"I see the look in your eye," Matt said. "Taking the lead doesn't mean running off and the rest of us follow."

"I'm listening, cowboy."

"Taking the lead means doing what's right for your followers, and what you've got behind is a group of people and animals striving to end the day feeling content and unified."

I looked back. Maggie and Glad rode alongside each other in quiet conversation. Glad pointed out flowers and birds. Quinn and Dad soaked in the scenery, and Silas brought up the rear. His steely gaze focused on the McIntyre crew, the cast of misfits in my mind, out for a leisurely afternoon ride.

"Quit looking so worried. I'm not running. Today." I ran my fingers through Gypsy's mane.

"Hard telling with you, darlin'," Matt replied.

I trotted a few horse lengths ahead, then peered over my shoulder with a toothy smile.

"You're impossible."

"I wouldn't go that far. Challenging. Impossible, yet to be determined." I patted Gypsy, her hide warm from the sun.

Maggie and Cora made their way closer. "Let's not test the waters," she said. "Let's keep this ride at an easy pace *all* the way home."

"We will. The sisterhood will stick together."

"Yes, we will, for my mother's sake." Maggie tugged on the brim of her hat.

"I hear ya'." I pulled back on Gypsy until Glad caught up. I inhaled a long draw of air and eyed my posse, hoping I wore pride like Dad. "We're heading home, Gladiola," I called out with a nod to the horizon.

"Yeehaw," she hollered. "And I've thought it through."

"Thought what through?" I responded while circling around.

"It's time I sold my house. John, how would you feel about taking this old bird in?"

Maggie pulled back on Cora's reins. "What did you say, Mom?"

"It's time I joined my crew. With all the rearranging going on here, I thought I'd let you know before you got too situated in that new office of yours, daughter."

CHAPTER 22

I'D DELIVERED JUSTIN'S dinner to the bunkhouse as requested. He was taking advantage of how I felt, and I'd let him if it meant making amends. "Hey there. Got some pulled chicken, bean salad, bread, and a couple slices of Glad's orange marmalade cake." I shuffled up the steps and set the tray on the table. "You missed a great ride this afternoon."

"Thanks," he said.

"When's this moping going to end?"

"Maybe never," he muttered.

I popped the top of the cold beer, uncovered his dinner, and handed him the fork. "I'm prepared for your lifetime of sorrow. I suppose this can't be any different than a child's a temper tantrum." I sat in the ladder-back chair across from him and propped my feet up on the railing. "Glad says she's selling her Michigan property and moving in."

"Where's that put you? We don't need no woman in the bunkhouse, although you'd fit right in."

"Does Silas really sit out here and play sad tunes before lights out?"

Justin nodded.

"What else does he do?"

"He sings in the shower, but you probably could've guessed that. He makes his bed every morning, says his prayers, and writes poetry in a journal. He's a serious reader, too. Likes the classics."

"Thanks for the lowdown. It'll help me get to know him better, but if he picks me up again, I'm docking his pay." I eyed Justin's plate. "You gonna eat that? If not, I could use seconds."

"Yes, I'm gonna eat my dinner. You gonna stay here and bug me?"

"Do you want me to?" I crossed my ankles and settled in for the long haul.

"Not especially. I'd like to eat in peace," he said.

I stood. "Any word from your brother?"

"Nope." He looked up from beneath his lashes. "You gonna ask me about Tristan every time I see you?"

I nodded. "Why'd you stay?" I leaned against the railing and took in the dusky sky promising a starry night.

He slugged down the rest of his beer then stood

beside me.

"I'm listening."

"Well, it's about time." He lifted his chin and crossed his arms over his chest.

"I deserved that."

"You gonna keep taking my jabs and delivering me breakfast, lunch, and dinner?"

I felt his stare upon me. "Yes." I faced him. "Why'd you stay?" I took another beer from my other shirt pocket and gave it to him.

He popped the top. "Because I like it here. I don't want to work anywhere else. When I weighed the pros and cons—and to be clear, you weren't on the list of pros at the time—the pros outweighed the cons, and I figured I'd be mad at myself if I left. I've followed my brother before. Doesn't always turn out good for me. He's tougher than I am, can handle harsher landscapes and scrappier men. I'd rather know what I'm getting into before I sign on." He ran his fingers through his hair.

"I meant it when I said I'd do anything to get him back here to work," I said.

"Would you quit working for your father?"

I pretended to laugh. "No." I crossed my arms over my belly. "You'd better eat. If you hear from your brother, let me know."

"Chloe—"

I skipped down the steps. "Yeah."

"Will you bring me breakfast tomorrow?"

"Sure thing, Justin."

"Dang, you must really feel bad. This whole baby thing is working in my favor."

"Glad to hear it, because I'm not so sure it is for me. Living under the same roof as my parents and Glad with a newborn won't exactly make for a house of harmony." I tucked my hands in my pockets. "I should get going. I'll see you in the morning."

THE TRUCK WAS parked outside the barn, and something furry moved in the front seat.

"Got a surprise," Matt said, tugging at my hand. "Come on."

Our boots scuffled in unison as we hurried to the truck. The pointy-eared canine poked its snout out the open window.

"Is that what I think it is?"

"Yep. You're going to love her."

My breath caught in my chest. I opened the passenger door with a smile of approval. The shaggy herding dog jumped up on me, her paws planted on my thighs. "What's your name?" I scratched her head. "She's so pretty. A miniature collie with cattle dog coloring."

"That's exactly what she is. And probably something else we don't know about. Her name is Lola."

Lola sat at my feet. Her pink tongue waggled. "I like her name." Matt appeared pleased with his surprise. "She's totally a Lola." I knelt to stroke her shaggy fur. "You gonna help us with those snarky cattle?"

She let out a woof.

"Thought you'd approve. There's something special about her, you know."

"Where'd you get her?" I sat on the ground, and she crawled into my lap. Her nose touched mine, and she gave me a slurp.

"Animal shelter in Bozeman." He paused. "I've been looking for a dog who needs a home. Was thinking I'd break down and spend the cash on a purebred but ran across this girl."

"Gosh, I can't believe someone gave her up. She's so sweet. I love her," I said.

Matt reached down and grabbed my hands. With one tug, I was in his arms again. His hands rested on the small of my back. Lola sat at our feet as though she had been ours since she was a pup. "Good surprise, cowboy."

"I thought if I couldn't win you over with my good looks and charm, a dog might work."

Matt's brow creased; he was digging deep into the pit of his soul where he kept the fragile parts of him. I had a place like that, too. I supposed we all did.

"You're the mother of my child."

"Stop," I said.

"Why? You're gonna have to live with it sooner or later. You've made it clear ranching comes first. Open your eyes, Chloe. The people who care are with you, day in and day out. We're just adding one more." He paused. "What do you want, Chloe? Do you want a family, or are you going to fly by the seat of your pants hoping to catch the gold rings as you're flying by? At the end of the day, you might have a hand full of gold, but what'll it mean without having someone to share it with?"

I held his gaze. My loss of words was deafening.

He kicked at the stall door, took off his hat, and raked his fingers through his hair. "I want to give you things, Chloe. I'm not sure I can, because you're determined to forge a path of your own with me on your heels, not by your side. You wanted to ride regardless of my concern. You rode.

We haven't really spoken about the position your dad offered me. Reading minds usually gets me into trouble. And according to your dad, you'll be moving out soon. You haven't said a word."

"Where? I haven't spoken to anyone about moving out. What do you know that I don't?"

Matt opened the stall door. He tossed one of the bales of hay from the aisle into the empty stall. Then he tossed another bale into the stall. This time with more heft. "Nothing. My point wasn't you moving. Everything revolves around you." He tossed in a third bale with a grunt. "You're not going anywhere, Chloe. This ranch is your life. Baby or no baby. Single, attached, or not attached, and I choose those words carefully."

I folded my arms over my chest and glared at him. I didn't think I had ever been cross with Matt until now.

"You hide behind uncertainty. Being a momma can't be much different than riding, roping, corralling, and tending to the animals," he said. "You're pretty good at all those things."

"I'm great," I said, kicking at the last bale of hay. Matt moved it before I made contact. I lost my balance and caught myself on the stall door.

"We all lose our footing. We're all tested. Lord knows," he grumbled under his breath. "Let's not do this.”

“I’m not sure I started this.”

“Doesn’t matter who started it.” He sat on the last bale of hay and patted the seat next to him. “I’m frustrated. Just not sure where I fit in. Bickering with you wasn’t my intention.”

His words hung between us like wet laundry in a rainstorm. “This isn’t what I want either,” I said.

“I know, but maybe it’s what you need. Look—” He paused. “I’ve tried to be gentle here. We all have limits.”

“What does that mean?”

He rubbed his jaw and put up his hands.

“And you wonder why marriage and children aren’t on my bucket list. This is why. I loathe fighting. All it leads to is an end.”

The corner of his lip turned up. “So you say. I beg to differ.” He paused. “A disagreement doesn’t mean the road stops. There doesn’t have to be a cliff. Come on, Chloe.”

Lola turned in circles and jumped when Matt reached into his pocket. “She thinks you have a treat.”

Lola sat at his feet and pawed at his shin. “I don’t.” He scooped her up and cradled her in his arms. “Sometimes, they’re just looking for attention, like the rest of us. Aren’t you, pretty, girl?”

He walked into the office.

Huckleberry poked her nose out of her stall. Coal's scamper into the barn was followed by my dad's slow stride. By the scowl on his face, he'd heard my conversation with Matt.

"How much did you hear?" I set my jaw and bit the inside of my cheek.

"Enough." He pushed his hat back from his brow. "He's right, you know. One argument doesn't mean the road ends. It means you have to stop. Think matters through, then choose a direction. Hopefully, it'll be together in some regard."

"I can't promise that. No one can." I walked to the other end of the barn and straightened the pile of saddle blankets heaped on the tack box.

"Maybe not. But it can lead to something greater, too. Breaking up with your mom was difficult even if it was mutual. Relationships are hard work. Period."

Lola trotted out from the office without Matt.

With his hands tucked in his pockets and his chin to the ground, Dad went into the office and shut the door behind him.

I scratched Lola's belly and told her she'd be great with the cattle and horses. Matt thought he needed a shield, and she was it.

Coal leaped upon the blankets and snuggled in. I sat on the tack box and stroked her silky fur. She raised her head long enough to investigate the sniff making her whiskers twitch. Satisfied, she lowered her chin, and purred until she fell asleep.

"If I could curl up in a ball and shut out the world, I would. This is not how this day was supposed to end," I said to myself.

Maggie and Glad came into the barn. "I hear there's a new addition to the wrangling team," Maggie said.

Lola snapped to attention to greet them. She was the whole package, pink tongue, wagging tail, and obedient.

"She's gorgeous." Glad kneeled to pet her.

I let Coal snooze and turned my attention back to Lola. She was perfect, and I scolded myself for seeing her as a wedge. "I think Lola's supposed to teach me a lesson, or at least that's what I think Matt thinks. That's a lot of thinking." I rubbed my temples.

"So what if it is?" Maggie hesitated. "You're not exactly easy. You already know there's a price for independence. And if you get to keep Lola and learn something along the way, I'd say that's a win-win."

Matt and Dad came from the office.

"She'll make a great herder," Matt said. "She's kind of a mutt, but sometimes mutts make for the most loyal companions and hardest workers. She's cattle dog, sheltie, and who knows what else."

I watched Lola investigate the crowd, deciding character with friendly investigation. Matt's stare was no different. "I like the white patch of fur on her forehead and her black nose," I said. "Gives her personality."

"The dog could have three legs, be pink, and you'd love it." Glad linked her arm with Maggie's.

"Since the animals are all tucked in, I'm gonna hit the hay, too. We've got another busy day ahead of us tomorrow," Dad said.

"The road doesn't stop." Matt leaned against the doorjamb, saying his good nights to Maggie, Glad, and Dad.

Lola sat at my feet as if she'd been primed to watch over me. I knelt and gave her the attention she deserved her first night here and in all the days to come.

Before Dad left, he patted Matt on the back. "Goodnight, son."

"Goodnight," Matt replied. "I'll think about what you said."

I blew Glad a kiss, my delivery not as strong as it could have been. "I'll be in shortly," I said.

Glad pulled at the front of her coat. "Sure is a special place. Night, all."

When their voices had drifted into the darkness, Matt shut the office door. "You'll think about what? What was Dad referring to?"

He fiddled with his hat. "I don't think I should say."

"Great," I snapped.

"Fine. What do I have to lose?" He rubbed his jaw. "Let me preface this by saying, your dad's just trying to help."

Lola went into the empty stall and curled up on the tufted hay in the dark corner. Her soft snores filled the silence between us.

Matt went back into the office and returned with a yellow legal pad and a pencil. "Before we say goodnight, I want to show you something." He scribbled some numbers on the yellow legal pad.

"What do numbers have to do with anything?"

"See the top number?"

I nodded.

"That's the number of cattle the McIntyres have."

"That's more than I thought," I said.

"Your dad and I have been working the numbers." His tone filled with anticipation. "Those extra head of cattle belong to me. Whether I accept your dad's job offer or not, he's giving me a chance to build my own herd on your land."

"Yours? Guess your business degree is coming in handy after all." I'd failed to read the signs. My self-centered attitude didn't serve the change happening around me. "Lola's not a gift, is she?"

Matt sighed. "When you looked at her, I didn't have the heart to tell you she's a hired hand. *My* hired hand. I got her to help with the cattle I bought. They might not seem like much, but your dad's giving me an opportunity I can't turn down. You're not the only one with something at stake."

"Sounds like Dad's really priming you for the position. Have you told him you'd take it?" I didn't tell him how left out their relationship made me feel.

"That depends on you, Chloe."

When Matt took the paper and pencil back into the office, I breathed in the night air and shuffled off into the darkness.

CHAPTER 23

AFTER LAST NIGHT, I thought it'd be a good idea to keep my head down and my feelings to myself. Completing chores and breaking a sweat made me believe I had at least one part of my life under control. Making things right with Tristan was still on my radar and Matt's prospects overshadowed my thoughts of where I'd live when the baby came.

I'd stayed behind today to work in the barn and tend to the horses. A day of grooming, trimming tails, and mucking out stalls would do me good. It wasn't a day at the spa, but it was a day alone. And instead of a hot shower to unwind, I had my sights set on riding.

Brownie's tan speckles shone in the midday sun like brown pebbles under a rustling gray stream. Lola ran from the barn to greet me. "What are you doing here, girl? Thought you'd be out learning how to wrangle."

I unwound Brownie's reins from the hitching post. A jagged splinter of wood scraped the side of my hand. "Ouch." I inspected the blood coming to the surface and wiped it on my bandana.

I led Brownie to the mounting block and got on. The radio jabbed me in the lower back as I settled into the worn saddle, then headed up the trail to the ridge. An inkling of knowing better came over me, but I ignored the fact that I'd said I wouldn't ride alone. Brownie needed work, and an easy ride would do him good.

"You stay here, Lola." She sat. Her alert brown eyes eager to join me. "You tell them I'll be back soon." She whimpered, then settled down, resting her head on her front paws. Samson poked his nose from the barn with an irritated grimace, then meandered toward the house.

Brownie sauntered along the muddy path. Matt's words hung in the low branches scraping against my jacket. I hunched forward to avoid getting poked. He'd bought five cows and their calves. He brought on Lola to help him wrangle. He took steps forward while my ambitions had been derailed. Blue sky nudged its way through the canopy as we neared the first clearing. Brownie snorted and labored up the first incline. He wasn't the fastest horse, but he worked hard. "Come on, now. We're in this together. I'm not asking you to run."

I leaned forward, shifting my weight to ease the load. "I'm going to miss not riding when the time comes," I told him. He stopped on the trail then trotted to the open field. Sparse yellow and purple petals dotted the field like a Parisian painting. Static on the radio pierced the air, and Brownie kicked up his rear hooves.

"What's the matter?" I patted his neck. "You're not usually so sensitive. It's just the radio." Despite the prickle in his hesitation, he moved on with a nudge of my heels. "Come on," I urged. Brownie's ears twitched. "We're almost there." He stumbled. My body jerked backward, and I gripped the saddle horn.

"Just hold on. We've got this." But my voice was anything but convincing.

I scanned my surroundings. "Everyone has an off day," I told him. "Trust me, I should know. I've had more than my share." I reached into my saddlebag, feeling for the bear spray.

Brownie's ears went back, and the breeze died down. An eerie feeling washed over me in the surrounding silence. "What's got your hide standing on end, boy?"

With my finger on the trigger of the bear spray, we trotted to the other side of the meadow. He craned his neck, revealing a panicky gaze.

Brownie shook his head and whinnied. His front hooves left the ground before I knew it. I heard Matt's fierce voice on the radio asking me where I was. I held tight to the reins and squeezed Brownie with my legs.

Brownie squealed and bolted as soon as his front feet were back on solid ground. I wrapped my hand in his mane and held tight. My cowboy hat came loose and bounced against my back from the chum hooked to my collar.

I crouched low, trying to gain control. Brownie yanked free, his tug more forceful than any power I wielded. His hooves thundered through the narrow path to the next incline. "Stay with me," I yelled.

The snarl of a bobcat sent a shiver down my spine. I gripped the saddle horn with all my energy. When the cat leaped up, I wiggled my left foot free of the stirrup and kicked at it. I missed, then found my foothold.

Matt's voice blared over the radio again. I put my head down and trusted Brownie's instincts. He reared up. I crouched low, the tall grass a blur.

Matt's voice boomed over the sound of Brownie's thundering hooves. He and Trigger galloped behind me, closing the gap. Lola sprinted to the lead, her white canines bearing down.

Brownie and I made our way up the next rocky incline to the ridge. The banter of the cat's snarl and Lola's relentless growl came to an abrupt halt, then began again. Brownie stopped in his tracks near Grandpa's rosebush, throwing me forward against his neck.

I yelled Lola's name.

Panic crawled over me, leaving me cold and clammy. I loosened my grip from Brownie's mane and the reins. My white knuckles ached. Brownie craned his neck to see me. His hide was sleek with sweat.

"Ya!" Matt shouted. Trigger clomped up the rocky trail at a wicked pace. Lola's relentless barking and growl ceased.

I scanned the landscape through delicate evergreen needles that hung from the branches like shaggy bangs. I wiped my brow, put my hat back on, and gave Brownie a nudge. He shook off the excitement, and I patted his shoulder.

Matt and Trigger rounded the boulder in the center of the clearing on Grandpa's ridge. Matt dismounted and dropped to one knee. My heart tore open when I saw Lola lying in the grass. Matt's tight jaw and clenched teeth raised the hair on my neck.

I pulled back on Brownie's reins and swung my

leg over the back of the saddle. When my feet hit the ground, I fell forward and caught myself on Matt's shoulder. Lola's panting subsided as her pleading gaze intensified.

Matt reached into his back pocket for his bandana. He wiped the blood from his hand then pressed the red cloth against Lola's side.

"Is she going to be okay?" Guilt slithered through my veins, leaving me cold. "I didn't mean for this to happen," I whimpered. Her tail lay limp against the ground.

"Thank goodness she was here," Matt said. "What the heck happened?"

"Brownie got spooked and ran." I sat down and cradled Lola's head in my lap. My shoulders quaked. "I'm so sorry."

"What are you doing up here by yourself, Chloe?"

The words lodged in my throat. I contemplated saying nothing. "Brownie needed exercise, a little work, and I wanted to be alone in my special spot."

Matt sighed. "We talked about not riding alone. You agreed not to."

"I thought it would be a leisurely ride."

Matt held me close. He scanned the tree line for the bobcat, but we both knew it had scampered off. "Good gravy, girl." Matt put his finger to my lips. "None of that matters right now. Are you hurt?"

"I'm fine, just scared."

"You're scared? If it weren't for Lola, who knows what would have happened to you and—" His voice broke. He pushed his hat back from his forehead and shook his head. "It could've been catastrophic."

"Is Lola going to be okay?"

"She's gonna need to see a vet. We'll have to get her back down the mountain. She can ride with me."

I leaned into Matt. The heat from his body penetrated my clothing. "I didn't mean to scare you."

Matt looked to the sky. "Winston, she is one tough nut," he said. "I bet you had your days with Ida May that weren't much different." He stood, walked to the rosebush, and plucked the lonely yellow bloom from the prickly overgrown bush. He handed it to me, and I rubbed it against my cheek.

Matt inspected Lola's side. "She's got three deep claw wounds here. This wasn't the kind of herding I had in mind. When she ran off, I followed. She wasn't coming home without you."

Lola whined and tried to get up when Matt touched her.

She licked the side of my face.

"Dang, girl, there ain't one animal on this ranch that isn't in love with you."

"I may not seem like it right this moment, but I can be rather charming," I said.

"Here, hold the bandana to Lola's side."

I held the cloth. Matt held my face in his hands. My belly turned over with his touch. His thumbs caressed my cheeks, then his mouth covered mine, and I melted into his kiss.

Leaning back, I held his gaze. "How mad are you?"

He ran his fingers down my neck and inside the collar of my shirt. His fingers found my racing pulse.

Static littered the air. I reached for the radio on the back of my belt. Maggie's voice came across loud and clear. "Yes, I'm fine," I answered. "Matt and I will be home soon."

"I want to hear Matt's voice," Maggie demanded.

"You've got at least two of us to answer to now, and I suspect more." He took the radio. "I'm here, Maggie. We'll be home shortly. Can you call the vet? We'll be taking our friend Lola in. She's okay, too, but she needs some attention."

"Copy," Maggie responded.

Matt squatted next to Lola and supported her head. I pushed myself up from the ground and shook out my legs and walked over to the rosebush. I listened for my grandpa's words in the breeze that had kicked up. Threatening clouds rolled in, with a sudden biting chill. I knelt beside Grandpa's memorial and traced his name on the stone cross.

My stomach cramped. I looked over my shoulder at Matt, who was soothing Lola. Another hard pinch radiated through my abdomen. Matt continued to coddle Lola, and I said nothing about the pain I felt.

I stood on the ridge and took in the valley view. It was grander than any postcard. Autumn colors speckled the landscape with the faintest existence. I tucked my hands into my front pockets and balled up my fists when Matt called my name. "I'm coming," I told him even though I needed another moment to myself.

Matt watched me walk toward him.

"What's the matter?" he asked.

"Nothing, just feeling jumbled. Not exactly the ride I had in mind."

"You're telling me," he said, holding Brownie's

reins in my direction. "Want a boost?"

I nodded, but this wasn't the kind of *boost* I needed. Matt cupped his hands. I stepped into his laced fingers and swung my leg over the back of the saddle. Matt tightened the girth and checked my stirrups. His stern jaw and determination drew me in.

"I need your help." He picked up Lola. "I'm going to hand her to you. Can you hold her while I get back on Trigger?"

She whimpered in my arms. "You're gonna be okay." I cradled her close to my body. Streaks of blood stained her fur. Hopefully, the cat hadn't ruptured any of her internal organs. If Lola didn't survive, I didn't know how I'd live with myself.

Matt put his left foot in Trigger's stirrup and hoisted himself up with one swift movement. His thick fingers gripped the saddle horn. He had the hands of a rugged wrangler and the heart of a saint.

He slipped off his shirt and, using his bandana, jimmied a sling across the front of his body. With a grunt, he yanked on the knotted fabric. "That should hold," he said. Trigger nuzzled beside Brownie. Matt pressed his leg against my saddle, leaned over, and took Lola. "I got you, girl."

He could've been talking to either one of us.

Lola curled up against his body and lay still. "Apparently, I'm not the only one with a knack for animals," I said.

"That's because I'm big and cuddly."

He was right about that. "Lead the way home, cowboy."

"You got it. Keep your eyes peeled for that nasty cat, and keep the bear spray in hand."

This was going to be a long ride down the mountain.

CHAPTER 24

MATT NESTLED LOLA into the crate in the back of Maggie's SUV, shut the rear hatch, and checked to make sure it latched. "You sure you don't want me to go with you?"

"Lola and I will be fine," Maggie said. "Can you make sure Chloe is okay?" Maggie shot me a look, and I knew we'd talk when she returned.

"Sure will," he said.

I crossed my arms over my chest and went into the barn. I winced at the pinch in my lower back. Matt followed.

"What's the matter?" Matt asked.

"I don't know. I had this off feeling at the top of the mountain. It went away, but now I feel crampy."

"You're going to the doctor. Get your stuff," he ordered.

"I have to tend to Brownie and help you get Trigger cleaned up. I'll sit for a bit. I'm sure it's nothing."

"Yes, you'll sit in the truck while I drive. You

need to see a doctor. Pack a bag in case you have to stay. Someone else can take care of the horses." Matt called Justin on the walkie-talkie to give him a heads up that he was off the clock. Matt's jaw twitched, his dark gaze unwavering.

"I'll drive you up to the house."

Matt put his arm around my waist and helped me into the truck. He leaned across my body and buckled me in, then ran around the front of the truck.

"We're only going to the house."

"Wear the seat belt, Chloe."

I did as I was told. The pain subsided in the five-minute drive to the house. "I'm okay," I said.

"You're still going. You had one heck of a ride, and we're not taking any chances."

Matt helped me up the front steps and into the quiet house. I stopped to feel the smooth, heavy banister beneath my grip and took the stairs slowly.

"I'll call ahead," he said.

Matt went to Dad's office to use the phone. Dread and regret made for a heavy load up the stairs. I stopped on the landing and took a deep breath, then went to my bedroom. I wanted to lie down, put my feet up, and forget the afternoon's events.

The radio poked me as I leaned back onto the bed. I finagled it from my belt and called my dad. "Can you come up to the house for a few minutes? It's kind of an emergency," I told him.

Matt's footsteps echoed in the hallway outside my door. The mattress tugged beneath my body when he sat next to me on the edge of the bed. He put the palm of his hand on my forehead. "You're overreacting," I said.

"I don't think I am."

"Dad's on his way up. He's a doctor. Remember?" I kicked off my boots and curled up in the downy comforter. "If only college had trained us for real life. Don't you think it's funny how no one uses their respective degrees around here anymore?"

"You're impossible. Now lie still."

"Not a problem. All I need is a nap," I insisted. "And a minute to relieve my bladder. It really feels strange." I rubbed my belly.

"You don't know what you need," Matt said.

"Hey, who are you to tell me what I need?" I quit sniping when I heard Dad in the hallway.

Matt stood and made room for my father. "She's having pains in her back and abdomen," Matt said.

Dad felt my forehead with the back of his

hand. "You don't have a fever. What happened?"

I grimaced. "I'm sure Matt will fill you in later. You can lecture me then."

Dad looked at Matt, then back to me. "Did you fall?" he asked.

"No."

"Do you feel sick?"

"Nope."

"Get thrown from your horse?"

"Not exactly." I sighed.

"Are you bleeding?"

"I don't know. I didn't use the bathroom when I came in. I wanted to lie down."

"Please, go to the bathroom and check."

Dad supported my head and helped me up.

Matt gestured for me to move quicker.

"I'm going." I left the room.

"She and Brownie were chased by a bobcat. She had quite the ride," Matt told my dad.

"Did she fall from her horse?"

"I can hear you two. No, I did *not*," I called from the bathroom doorway. I pulled off my socks and slid my feet across the cool tile floor after shutting the door.

Tiny specks of blood stained the crotch of my underwear. I sat on the toilet and rested my head in my hands. For the first time, the thought of losing the baby weighed heavily on my conscience. Blessing in disguise? Or would this be a lesson to push me to reevaluate my life's dos and don'ts? I ran my hands over my belly before standing to get dressed. The slightest baby bump, no bigger than a bloated abdomen protruded. What had I done?

I sucked in a breath, then zipped up my jeans. When would Maggie's purchase arrive? I'd welcome the stretchy denim.

I washed my hands with warm, sudsy water, leaned closer to the mirror. I should've opted for the hot shower after doing chores.

Matt was standing in the hallway when I opened the door.

"There's a hint of spotting." I waddled back to my room and sat on the edge of the bed with Dad. Matt followed. "Can I please lie down?" I begged. Dad tucked a pillow beneath my feet.

"Chloe, lay back. How much blood was there?"

I covered my face with my arm. "Just a little, but I think it's stopped."

Dad ran his hand over my abdomen. "This is nothing to mess around with. How bad is the cramping?"

"My muscles get tight. Big pinches that make me want to double over. Not sure if it's a cramp or a muscle pulling."

"Has it stopped?"

I smoothed the fabric from my shirt over my belly. "Yes. Unzipping these pants was a major relief."

"Let's see what your doctor says. Sounds like you had a wild ride. What were you doing up there alone?"

"No one was around. I needed to clear my head. Thought it'd be a slow-paced, easy ride." I paused. "Fine. I'll stay off a horse for a while." I ran my hand across my face and placed it behind my head.

"Good idea. Your doctor will help you set the guidelines," Dad said, patting my hand. "Sounds like Lola is a hero."

"Yes, she's some hero. Matt wasn't half bad himself," I said.

"You're welcome." He zipped up the duffel. "Let's go."

"I didn't pack anything." I lifted my head from the pillow.

"I did." The corner of his mouth lifted.

Matt and my dad exchanged looks. I propped myself up on my elbows. "What?" Dad took my hand and helped me sit up. Matt put my flip-flops on my feet.

"Call me if you need me," Dad said.

Matt took off his cowboy hat. "John, I'd like to stay with Chloe tonight if it's okay with you. Thought I should ask since we might be getting back late."

"What about Glad?"

"Don't worry about me," she answered, stepping into the room. "I've been lurking in the hallway. From what I understand, Trout has an extra room and there's a pullout downstairs, I'll be fine. Now go."

"Staying over is a good idea so you're close if she needs something," Dad answered.

I fell back upon my pillow. "Geez. When won't I be outnumbered?"

"I'm gonna pretend you didn't say that." Dad raised his brow at Matt.

"I'm going to grab a bag. I'll be back," Matt replied. "John, can you let Justin and Silas know I'm off the clock?"

"Sure thing, son. Get going. I'll get Chloe into the truck."

DAY HAD TURNED to night, and the moon lit the road home. I rolled down the window. The cool surge of air was refreshing after four hours in the emergency room. Matt had asked me if I wanted food, and I declined. The only thing I wanted was to be in my own bed. "You sure you want to stay with me tonight?"

"Yes." He ran his fingers through his hair.

"Don't you think it'll be weird?"

"It's not exactly what I had in mind, but it's the right thing to do." Matt's sincerity was a direct delivery. "You've got two double beds. You won't even notice I'm there. And if you want something, I'm your guy. And before you say anything, I've noticed how you're letting Justin have his way with you. He's not going anywhere."

"I want to make sure," I said.

"How you gonna top being at his beck and call the next time you ruffle his feathers?"

"I don't know. I'm sure I'll figure it out when the time comes. Right now, I'm worried about the baby." I rested my hands on my belly.

"Me too." He gripped the steering wheel tighter. "We'll follow up with Dr. Hennessey in the morning. The exam and ultrasound appeared normal. And the doctor said the blood could've been from the urinary tract infection you have."

"She also said sometimes they can't confirm a miscarriage immediately." The words weighed heavy on my mind.

"That's where Dr. Hennessey comes in. She'll do the proper follow-up tests and monitor you."

And Matt would have my back like he always did.

I SAT IN bed eating the turkey sandwich Matt made me while I showered and put on my pajamas. The trophies and old photos lining the shelves were mere evidence of a time long past. I didn't belong here anymore. Finding my way meant living on my own. Baby or no baby.

Matt peeked into the room. "I have something for you," he said. "There's a whiny dog out here who wants to bunk with her pack."

I sat a little taller. Matt padded softly across the wooden floor, carrying Lola on her bed. His flannel sleeping pants brushed against his bare feet. Samson watched from the doorway. His brow creased, and he lowered his gaze before waddling away when Matt lowered Lola next to the guest bed. She was cleaned up and had a bandage wrapped around her belly.

"I don't think Samson's a fan."

"He'll come around." Matt picked Lola up and laid her beside me.

I ran my fingers through her soft fur. "I'm so

glad you're okay. You're my hero."

"Mine too," Matt uttered into her shaggy fur as he nuzzled his face close to hers.

I scratched Lola's ears and rubbed my nose against hers. Her sloppy kisses were in sync with her tail thumping against the lofty comforter.

I slid beneath the covers, and Matt stroked my hair.

"You gonna let me in?" he asked. "I think that was your dad's plan when he asked me to keep an eye on you."

"Thought you wanted me to have my space. And I *think* you misinterpreted my dad's plan." I pointed to the bed across the room. "You'd have it all to yourself. Besides, I've already got company. Right, Lola?"

"That's why I brought her bed." He picked her up, then returned her to the dog bed. She curled up and went to sleep.

"I believe there's a vacancy now," he said.

"Fine." I scooted over, and Matt crawled in next to me. He put his arm across my pillow, and I snuggled close, then rested my head on his burly cowboy chest. His cotton T-shirt was cool against my skin. "Thanks for staying with me," I whispered.

"Thanks for letting me."

I breathed him in. His chest rose and fell like the moments of the day. "I've been thinking."

"You're always thinking. We can talk tomorrow. It's late." He switched off the light on the nightstand. The blue-black night sky drifted over my room on the heels of the sandman I imagined living in the starry sky outside my window.

I propped myself up on one elbow and stared at his profile. "I should move out and get my own place."

"That's up to you."

I tossed and turned and scrunched up my pillow the way I liked it. "Why aren't you pressuring me to get hitched?"

"Because sometimes, hog-tying and roping can make an animal mighty furious."

"That's flattering." I rested my hand on his stomach.

"All I'm trying to say, and not very well, is that pressuring you won't help our relationship. I'm not sure where this baby is taking us, but I do know things will be better if we work together. And let's face it, neither one of us is ready for marriage under these circumstances."

"There might not be a baby or *any* circumstances after today."

Matt held me close, then kissed my forehead. I

ran my fingers down his jaw and across his chin. The moonlight caught the dimple in his cheek. "You're one fine cowboy."

"I'm going to be the best man I can be—if you'll let me."

"What if we lose the baby?" My heart pinched.

"With or without the baby, being with you feels right."

Matt rolled over and fluffed the pillow before saying goodnight. His soft breaths turned to soft snores.

"'Night, Matt. Thanks for having my back." I pulled the covers up to my chin and watched the moonlight dance across the room. As exhausted as I was, I knew it would be a sleepless night.

CHAPTER 25

THREE WEEKS HAD passed. I'd seen Dr. Hennessey twice. She'd done an ultrasound during the last visit and reassured me the pregnancy should progress normally. She'd also suggested I give riding a back seat to rest. The infection had cleared up, and I was feeling healthy and back to my normal self.

I'd transitioned into a new wardrobe of stretchy denim, the give in the fabric much more comfortable. I'd have to shop again when I really grew. Maggie, Glad, and I had gone shopping for some cute tunics and a winter coat I'd be able to zip well into the spring. I'd tried on boots but couldn't bring myself to buy or break in a new pair.

Matt and I had gone about our daily business without too much distraction. Dad gave me bookwork to do to help fill the voids. I'd driven out to the pasture each day to soak in the wide-open land and think about what I wanted, what was best for me, Matt, and the baby. Leaving my dad out of the equation proved difficult at times, but I was learning how to find an acceptable equilibrium between business and my personal life.

Grounded had a whole new meaning. My restless impulses had been stinted by this transition I navigated. And as much as I craved to feel a saddle beneath my backside, riding would have to wait for the time being. In the quiet work hours of sitting at Dad's desk, tending to the animals, and light chores, I found myself milling around the original barn, reading by the fireplace, or following Maggie around when she was out photographing the countryside. She'd helped me buy a new camera and was teaching me how to use it.

I leaned against the split rail fence and stuffed my hands into the pockets of my denim jacket, nuzzling my chin into the shearling collar, warding off the chill in the air.

The horses lingered in the corral without rustling a blade of grass or speck of dirt. I kicked at the ground with the toe of my scuffed, worn-out boots I refused to give up.

Trout emerged from the barn. He leaned on the fence next to me, his mouth lined with worry.

"What's the matter, cowboy?"

"You know why I'm here?" he asked with a click of his tongue and twitch of his jaw.

I shook my head. "Why are you here? Shouldn't you be out with the others?"

"Not today, no thanks to you. Here I am."

"Did you draw the short straw again?"

The corner of his lip curled. "Nope." He started to light a cigarette, then put it away. "I've never had children. Never been married, but from the first time I laid eyes on you, I knew we were kin. I told your daddy I'd keep an eye on you. We're spending the day together whether you like it or not."

I smiled and played with the loose string inside my pocket. "Normally, I'd buck at the offer to have a chaperone." I watched the mirrored clouds drift across the glassy surface of the pond.

"This is no offer." Trout grunted then rested his foot on the fence rail.

"I don't mean to be a burden."

Trout dipped his head low to the top rail and peered into the distance, a place I couldn't see and probably wouldn't understand without the passage of time.

"No need to apologize. We all have our moments, and I have a confession to make. I never draw the short straw," he said.

"I've always had a soft spot for you, too. But I think you already know that." I rested my head on his shoulder.

"I do."

"Just making sure, cowboy."

"I saw the look in your eye when the men rode out this morning." His words trailed off like the first sprinkling of snow melting away.

"I promise I won't get on a horse." His hair and moustache were as white as fresh cotton, his dark eyes, serious and soulful. He was more than a ranch hand. We'd both known it since the day we met.

He smirked. "It's gonna take more than an old man to hold you down. Ain't nothing I'm gonna say to fertilize the common sense buried deep inside you."

"You sure do know how to charm a girl."

"You can't tame a wild animal's instincts, and you can't squelch a determined woman's desire. And that's what you are, a grown woman. And like I said before, I'm an old man."

"With wise wings to hide beneath when I doubt my sense of direction," I said.

"You've always been my favorite around here. Ain't never told you that. If I had a daughter, I'd want her to be like you. Ain't nothing wrong with a little sass."

Pride pushed my shoulders back, and I nudged

Trout. "So what's on your agenda? Dad's already given me a list."

Trout pulled out the cigarette from his pocket. "Guess I won't be smoking these while you're around." He tucked it back in his pocket. "I've had a lot on my mind lately. Mostly, you. And it's time I build my own place. Your grandparents would want you to have the house."

"That's a sweet gesture, but it doesn't seem right to take your home," I said.

"It belongs to you. I've just been the caretaker, making sure it was ready for you when the time came. And it's time. We all have to move on at some point."

His gaze met mine, the lines around his mouth etched deep.

"Besides, I have a secret."

"I bet you have lots of secrets." I batted my eyelashes at him.

"Not telling secrets today, darlin', or any day." He put his pinky and his pointer fingers in his mouth and whistled as if he were calling in the cavalry. The horses lifted their heads and walked toward us. Samson poked his head from the barn and barked. "I've been working the land since I was a boy. Spent most of it with Winston."

I liked how my grandpa's name rolled from

Trout's tongue. It sounded rough yet sentimental. "So what's the secret?" I rested my arms on the top rail of the fence.

"Thanks to your granddaddy, I can build my own house. Been stashing my pay away for years. I'm building a cabin near the river not too far from here." Trout pointed to a clearing beyond a patch of evergreens on the far side of Grandpa's house. "I'll be able to walk out my door and be right where I want to be. And when I get too old to mount a horse, I'll have the river to keep me company. It's far enough away from your place to give us all some room, but close enough to watch you raise a family."

I couldn't imagine Trout slowing down.

"Your daddy and I have it all worked out. You've got no excuses for not starting your own life. By the way, I put another stack of books next to the fireplace when you're ready."

"You always did play hardball when you had to."

"Never thought this time would ever come." He smoothed down his moustache.

"I know what you mean." The breeze picked up. Shallow ripples floated across the pond's surface, and the clouds moved swiftly overhead. "I wish Father Time would dig his heels in and slow the clock. Not just for me but for all of us. I don't like it when you talk about getting older." I rested my forehead on my clasped hands. Gypsy grazed near the fence line, keeping an eye on me.

"No one truly leaves here, darlin'. You know that." He paused. "I'll be in the trees. I'll be in the wind riding at your back. I'll be watching over you. Like your granddaddy and Ida May."

"You better," I said.

"I wouldn't be anywhere else."

"Good. Now that we have that settled, I'm in no hurry to move in."

"Now it sounds like you're talking about Matt," Trout said.

"I guess I kind of am. I don't like when I can't see the future. It's cloudy. I want reassurance."

"The rising sun brings the running of the horses, blue skies, and fresh beginnings. There's always a road, path, or calling. We're stuck in perpetual motion whether we want to be or not."

I picked at the splinters hanging from the fence rail. "You ever love anybody?"

"Yep," Trout replied.

Trout's stoic expression warned me his memories were closer to the surface than I would have expected.

"Suppose you don't want to tell me about it."

"Nope." He clenched and unclenched his jaw.

"Bet you wish you were herding cattle right about now," I said.

"Yep," he said with a grunt.

"Maggie can keep watch if you think you're gonna buckle under the pressure."

"She's not around today. She's out doing something for that book of hers."

"Oh." I stuffed my hands back in my pockets. "It's okay. I don't want to talk about it either."

"Good." He tucked his hands in his pockets, too.

The sun poked through the cloud cover. I held my chin to the warming light. "You gonna make me a cowboy lunch? I'm hungry." I shifted my weight; it was too early to eat.

"Nope. You're in charge of making lunch."

"Oh, so there is a list," I said.

Trout nodded. "More like a hidden agenda. So far, we're doing pretty good."

"Wanna ride out to the pasture and check on the guys?" I stroked Gypsy's neck.

Trout narrowed his gaze. "Only if I can drive," he said.

"Fine. Have it your way."

"If you insist, but we're not staying out there long. You need to get your feet up, according to that beau of yours."

"Good grief." I turned on a heel and walked toward the new pickup truck dad and I picked out together. I opened the passenger door and climbed in. Trout made sure I buckled up.

He walked around the front of the truck, opened his door, then ducked his head and slid into the driver's seat. "You had that moustache your whole life?" I asked, studying his profile.

"Yep." He stared straight ahead and turned the key in the ignition.

"I like it. I bet she did, too, whoever she was," I said.

"We ain't talking about that."

"Fine." I sighed. "You're no fun."

"I know."

I placed the palm of my hand on the window. The glass fogged up around my fingers. I put my hands in my lap and stared through the hazy outline. The gravel crunched beneath the tires as we rolled slowly down the drive toward the timber gateway marking our property.

"You got a beef with all women?" I blurted out.

"No, just the good ones."

I laughed.

"Including you," he mumbled through his

twitching moustache.

"What did I do?" I took off my hat and laid it on the seat between us. "Dang."

The road was smooth, and the ride was quiet.

"Hey, you missed the turn," I said, peering out the rear window.

"I know. Sometimes we miss the turns in life. Sometimes we miss the turn on purpose. No sense in looking back."

I turned around. "Where are we going?"

"To get some lunch."

"Thought I was cooking."

"Yep, me too, but then I thought about the peanut butter and jelly sandwich you'd make me and figured we'd better get some real cowboy food at the diner up the road."

"Good choice. I'm gonna get a slice of pecan pie and ice cream."

"Only if you eat a square meal," Trout jawed.

"Some things never change," I uttered under my breath.

"No, darlin', they don't—even if you think they do."

Trout held the door to the diner open. "Thanks, cowboy." I sauntered in, taking in the scents of homemade food on a hot griddle, fresh bread, and the profile of a wrangler I had a beef with.

"I'll be sitting at the bar. I think it's best you handle this on your own." The corner of Trout's mouth lifted.

I walked over to the booth beneath the buffalo head. "Excuse me, is this seat taken?"

Tristan looked up with a hard swallow.

"Don't mind if I do." I sat down across from him before he could answer. "Justin said you haven't been in touch."

He pushed mashed potatoes around on his plate, then set the fork down. "Not so much."

"Did he tell you I've been trying to get ahold of you?"

Tristan nodded.

I took the menu from the waitress and read the specials. "If you want me to leave you alone, all you have to do is say the word. I've got a date waiting for me at the bar."

Tristan glanced over his shoulder to acknowledge Trout.

"I won't stay long." I sipped the water from the dimple-textured plastic tumbler. "I want to apologize for my behavior. I wasn't fair to you. I'd like to blame it on the pregnancy, but I can't. I was trying to prove something to my dad, and I ended up losing the best man for the job in the long run.

Not to mention, I hurt your brother."

Tristan sat silent and held my stare.

"Okay then. This was a good talk." I paused. "I'm really sorry, about a lot of things."

I asked the waitress if Trout and I could sit on the other side of the restaurant so Tristan could have his space. When she gestured for me to follow her, Tristan put his hand on my arm.

"Wait." His gaze met the waitress's. "Could you give us a minute?"

"Sure, sugar," she said. "You let me know when you're ready."

"Thank you." Tristan pushed his shoulders back and took a deep breath. "Justin says you're not riding for awhile."

"So he told you about the scare with the baby?" Guilt slithered through me. I hadn't wanted this pregnancy, and the man sitting across from me would trade the world to have his son by his side.

He nodded. "I'm glad you're going to be okay." He clenched his jaw and hesitated. "That day in the truck when I told you about Vivian and James. I left out part of the story. We'd planned to have a day together, but the rancher I was working for called me to work and Vivian and I'd had a fight. She'd taken James to soothe his disappointment." He shook his head. "I should've been in that car. I should've been driving." His words came hard and harsh.

"Oh, Tristan."

"I don't know why I had to say that to you, but I did. You weren't the only one being a jerk. Justin told me how nice you people were and how you'd understand. Said you'd let me be me, and I lost me when I lost my family. And this is who I am right now. I'm hoping in time I might feel better about myself." He put on his wide-brimmed hat, placed some money on the table, and left.

"Me too," I whispered to myself.

CHAPTER 26

TROUT HELD THE diner door for me. "I still don't understand how you knew Tristan would be here."

"I told you, a cowboy doesn't talk about his women. Now, I'm gonna tell you, you don't need to know how I knew Tristan would be here. Besides, I have something else to show you before we head home."

"Fine," I mumbled.

"Do you good to remember you don't need to know everything. Knowing everything clogs the brain. You'd do better filling that curiosity with a little faith."

"Noted. Let's go."

The ride home was a quiet one. With a full belly and my load a little lighter, I took in the scenery until Trout drove down a road I hadn't noticed before. "Hey, this is on our property."

"Settle down. Your daddy knows about the dirt cut-in."

We drove through a grove of pines to a clearing

near the river where a crew of men and machines worked.

"My place won't be fancy like your daddy's. Bought a defunct log cabin in Virginia that's being transported here next week. Belonged to a family long before your time—and mine. Times were changing and the original owner packed up his young son, and they left hoping to find a better life. Literally walked and worked their way to Michigan in the late 1880s. The boy grew up and thought about that trip with his daddy every day after leaving home to build barns and raise a son of his own. One day, he took that son back to Virginia when he was a teenager. That young man grew up with his daddy's, grandaddy's, and great-granddaddy's stories inside him. Saving the cabin will keep the stories alive."

"You sure do know a lot about this family."

"Sure do. Cause it was my granddaddy doing the walking along his daddy's side. No taller than his daddy's waist. When I found out the cabin was still standing, I bought it, called a company to disassemble it, and bring it here. The builders will reconstruct it and remodel the inside." He hooked his thumbs in his belt loops. "Won't be truly done until spring."

"You've been working on this project for

awhile. Haven't you?"

"Yes, ma'am." The smile widened beneath his thick moustache. "And no, I ain't gonna tell you how long. It's something I've always wanted to do." He waved to a man carrying a chain saw. "Just wanted you to know, your grandaddy's house will be vacant. Whether you choose to live there is your business. When my place is done, they'll be a trail from my yard to yours. I suspect you'll be running away from time to time."

I nudged him with my shoulder. The breeze kissed my neck, and I knew Ida May had sent him to watch over me. "You ready to take this gal home?"

Trout perked up, and his eyes lit with a twinkle I hadn't seen before.

"What? Why are you looking at me that way?"

He shook his head. "You're the spitting image of Ida May. You even sound like the woman. Lord, have mercy."

"Then I guess we better be getting along." I patted him on the back with a smile.

"Thanks for lunch, kid. You take the truck. I'll find my way when I'm done here."

"You're welcome. Your cabin will be great. Your Daddy and Granddaddy would be proud." I scanned the clearing, imagining Trout's dream.

"And hey, thanks for the compliment."

I WENT INTO the old barn Grandpa had built with the original 617 house. I climbed the dusty staircase to the second floor and pulled on the chain to the bare bulb fixture at the top of the landing. Specks of dust danced in the light coming through the window at the far end of the long, rectangular loft. I sat in one of the antique wicker chairs. "Trout's moving on. You'd be real proud of him, Grandpa. Thank you for knowing I'd need him."

Dad shuffled up the stairs. "Am I interrupting?"

"Nope."

"Who you talking to, kid?"

"Grandpa." I noticed a hint of my granddad in my father's smile. "All my life, I thought Grandpa was my driving force because he was the one who held me in his lap, loved me unconditionally, and taught me that loving the land and animals is a special talent. I don't think that anymore." I fingered my tarnished belt buckle. The same belt buckle my grandfather wore day in and day out while tending our ranch. "Grandpa was the link. Ida May was making sure I found my place. She knew someone needed to fill her void and she chose me."

"She was a force to be reckoned with."

"How come you didn't tell me about Trout's cabin?"

"I didn't think it was my business to tell." He took off his hat and hung it on a nail.

"I'm glad he's decided to stay on the property. I can't imagine a day without him."

"Me either." Dad put his feet up on the old trunk. "Boy, I haven't been up here in ages. The gatherings and dances this place has known. If only the walls could talk."

I smiled at the nostalgia in his voice. "It's peaceful up here."

"Certainly is. A lot of memories."

"I'd like to hear your stories—all of them. I'll want to pass them along someday." I slid my bandana from my forehead and over the back of my head. I untied the knot in the fabric and folded it in my lap.

"Do you mind if we talk business first?" Dad asked.

"Not at all."

"Looks like you and Matt are moving in the right direction."

"Thanks, but I'm not sure my relationship with

Matt is business." I tucked loose hair behind my ears, thinking about Matt's philosophy about not roping and hog-tying another human being to get what I wanted.

"Well, actually it is. Matt says you and he haven't made a decision on the co-CEO offer. He and I had a heart-to-heart, as you call it. He's hesitant to take it." He paused. "He'd rather have a relationship with you than risk taking a job that might cause hard feelings. That's where the business comes in."

"It's not my place to convince him to do something he's not sure he wants to do. Or right for him." I knotted my hair at the nape of my neck.

"I'm not asking you to convince him to do anything. You've done a fine job keeping up the books these last few weeks and organizing from behind the scenes. And by the way, Silas is a never-ending source of resources, odd traits, and experiences. But his talents are a discussion for another time." He shook his head. "I want you to be my co-CEO. Matt knows I'm offering you the job."

I smiled. That's what I'd wanted all along. "I appreciate the offer, but no." I took my father's hand in mine. "I've been your righthand man all along and always will be whether I have a title or not. I thought proving my worth meant undermining my instincts in an effort to not be overlooked. As much as I've enjoyed sitting behind my daddy's desk for the past few weeks, I belong outside. I like being in the barn, working with my hands, riding with the wranglers."

"I thought you wanted to be co-CEO," he said.

"Me, too, but now I don't. Which brings me to—" I hesitated. "Living in Grandpa's house. I'd like to ask Matt to live with me when the time comes. How would you feel about that?"

"Chloe, you're an adult. The house is yours. We may reside on the same property, but it's time for you to live your own life." Dad sighed as he took in the dusty boxes labeled with Grandpa's scratchy handwriting, the discarded wagon wheels, and the odds and ends stored for a later time that never came.

"Funny how we pack things away, thinking we can't live without them. But somehow time replaces those memories with new ones of equal importance," I said, lacing my fingers with his like I did when I was a little girl. Of course, I was still growing and so was everybody else I loved.

"You sure you won't consider being my co-CEO?"

I shook my head with a smile.

"If you change your mind, you know where to

find me."

"Always, Dad." I looked down at my old boots, then back up to him. "And we've got other business to settle."

"Sure. What's on your plate?"

"I ran into Tristan at the diner. We had words, in a good way, I think." His hollow mood weighed heavy on my mind. "I know we've hired Silas on, but I'm going to need time to take care of me and the baby. I'm going to do my darndest to give this child everything *she* deserves."

Dad rested his elbows on the armrests of the chair. "She?"

I leaned back and rubbed my stomach. "Matt and I think it's a girl. As silly as this might sound, we think the people *upstairs* had a hand in this whole situation." I took the dusty frame holding my grandparents' picture from the side table.

"I like the way you think. And if the baby happens to be a strapping lad, I'll take that, too. I'll be the best granddad I can be."

"I know you will." I set the photo down. I'd take it with me, clean it up, and display it in my house when the time came. "How would you feel about hiring Tristan on?" I played with the frayed thread on my new jeans. "The boy could use a home, and something tells me he belongs here.

Besides, having Tristan here might give Matt the nudge he needs to consider being your co-CEO. I agree with you, he's the better person for the job."

Dad smiled. "You sure?"

"I'm sure." I stood and held out my hand to my father. He stood, shook my hand, then pulled me close for one of his best bear hugs.

"I love you, Chloe."

"Love you, too, Dad. Everything is changing. So much."

"Yes, it is. We have a lot to look forward to," he said.

"We'll work out the living arrangements until Trout's cabin is done. By then Maggie will need more creative space. She's really working up a storm. And your room will be perfect for Glad." Dad put his hat back on and tugged it tight across his brow.

I picked up the photo of Winston and Ida May. "Dad, I want you to know, I fully support you and Matt working together on growing his herd and ours. It's been his dream, and I don't want to be the reason he doesn't achieve it. And those Black Angus will certainly be easy to spot when we're rounding up the strays."

"You're not kidding. Matt's plan for growing a herd is solid, Chloe. And he's tickled pink that you've got his back."

"And as much as you didn't want to hear that your single daughter was pregnant, I'm glad I didn't lose the baby."

"Me too, sweetheart. And if you're going to live with someone, Matt's a fine someone."

"Thanks, Dad. And I'm grateful he has you to learn from. You haven't steered me wrong yet." I laughed. "Pun *not* intended. And if I forget to tell you, I'm having the time of my life living on this ranch." I kissed his cheek.

"You'll always be my Paris girl, Chloe."

"Dad—" Something inside me shifted, and I felt like a child tiptoeing through the house after a day of head-butting disagreements when I should've been in bed. I had to make things right.

"Yes, Chloe?"

"I want to apologize for the wrangler interviews, driving Tristan away, hurting Justin, and—well, being stubborn. From now on, I'll be straightforward with you. If I can lay it on the line with the business, I shouldn't be afraid of saying how I feel or telling you when I mess up."

"If you can be forthright, so can I." He lowered his gaze. "Trout says he's got some pointers for me when we don't see eye to eye."

"Oh boy. I bet he does." I pretended to hear

someone. "Do I hear Maggie calling us?"

Dad laughed, turned out the light, and ushered me down the stairs.

CHAPTER 27

MAGGIE AND GLAD had decked out the table with our best dishes, stemware, and fancy linens. Dad took his usual seat at the head of the table, Maggie at the opposite end. Silas, Quinn, Matt, Trout, and Tristan filled the empty seats. Justin's absence tugged at my heart. He'd fully moved in at the university, and we most likely wouldn't see him until classes ended in the spring. Glad called to me from the kitchen, and I went to see what she needed.

"Maggie says there's a vase of flowers in the mudroom. Would you mind carrying it into the dining room for me?" The corner of her mouth lifted with a mischievous smile, and she left the kitchen.

"Sure." When I flipped on the mudroom light, Justin was standing there.

"Is it okay if I join you for dinner, bosslady?"

"So there's no vase of flowers in here?"

"Nope. Only me."

I stepped closer to him. "I'd take you over a

bouquet any day.”

“Even if I don’t smell as nice?”

I laughed. “Even if you smelled like manure.”

He took off his hat and fiddled with the brim. “You must have it bad for me.”

“You know I do,” I said.

“I wanted to make sure we were good before I came in. I started feeling bad about making you wait on me until I left for school.” He smiled. “Well, not too bad.”

“I figured. You know, if we stand here long enough, Silas will have his way with the pot roast and we’ll be eating the trimmings, which would be a shame ’cause Maggie bought me these stretchy jeans. Now there’s plenty of room for seconds and dessert,” I said. “The past is the past. No need to rehash our foolishness.”

Justin hung his hat and coat on the hook, and we joined the rest in the dining room. Justin took a seat next to his brother and handshakes were reciprocated. I raised my water glass. “Before we eat, I want to say, this is the best-looking bunch of people in Montana. Life wouldn’t be worth living without you.”

“Here, here.” Matt raised his glass and the others followed.

Maggie stood and waited for the clinking of

glasses to cease. When her gaze met my dad's, her smile grew. "Since Chloe started us off with a toast, I have one too." She lifted her glass. "I didn't say anything before because I didn't want to jinx my news. The number of rejections I've received for my coffee table book could wallpaper this house." She paused. "Last week, I signed a contract, and I'm excited to say my collection of photos chronicling life on a Montana ranch will become a reality. The families, the barns, the animals, the plants, the seasons will be a published work."

"Here, here," Dad cheered.

The glass clinking commenced.

"I knew it would happen. Congratulations. We've got our own superstar. Couldn't be prouder." Glad's eyes brimmed with tears. She stood and hugged her daughter.

"You've been snapping pictures since the day you moved in. When will the book be out?" I asked.

"Sometime next spring," Maggie said, bubbling with excitement. "I can't believe it."

"I want an autographed copy," Glad said.

"Me too," I echoed.

"Copies for everyone." Maggie sat down and eyed the table. "We should eat before the food gets cold."

Glad put her hand on Maggie's as she reached for the cobalt blue bowl heaped with mashed potatoes. "Wait. Since we're all making announcements, I have one, too." She raised her glass. "I called my friend, Lois's son, today. My Michigan house is officially on the market. Montana, here I come."

Maggie and Dad raised their glasses, again. "Here, here," they said in unison.

"I hear you're good on horseback. Will you be wrangling, too?" Justin teased.

Glad laughed. "You never know, young man. And if I do, I want you by my side." She leaned over and kissed his cheek.

"Why, I do believe, I've never seen you turn so red," I said. "Looks like things are about to get interesting."

Everyone laughed. Justin pulled out Glad's chair and helped her get situated at the table. The good cheer and laughter warmed my heart.

DAD ASKED TROUT, Matt, and me to join him in his office after dinner. He shut the double doors and we all took a seat.

Dad sat and clasped his hands on the desk. "I

apologize for taking you away from the evening." His gaze met Trout's. "Chloe and I had a chat this afternoon, and I thought we should come together. Chloe, have you spoken to Matt since then? I don't want there to be any surprises."

"Yes, Dad. I told Matt I wasn't interested in being co-CEO. I prefer being in the trenches and on horseback. I appreciate you extending the offer to me, Dad. I really do. I thought having a title would mean something." I looked to Matt. "But Matt has the schooling. He's a better fit."

"You sure you don't want to accept the position, son?"

"No, sir. Not at this time," he answered.

"With that said, there'll be a day when I'll be looking for someone to fill those shoes. Matt, I believe you have what it takes to manage the ranch. If you change your mind, that door is open, and I won't hire anyone without asking you to step in first."

"Thank you. For now, I'd like to get my feet wet raising those Black Angus and see how they adapt." He sat taller. "I've done a bit of research. Should the opportunity arise, if you're up to it, there's promise in breeding them with the White Park."

Trout's smile wasn't hidden beneath his bushy

moustache. "Now that we have that settled. There's the matter of foreman."

"That's your job," I said.

"As much as I love relaying your daddy's orders and working from sunup to sundown, it's time I step down. I'm not getting any younger. Maybe wiser, but definitely not younger," he said.

Matt and I laughed.

"Your daddy's reassured me I'm welcome to ride alongside you when I get the hankering."

"No one can fill your boots." I took in his kindhearted expression mapped with experience and cowboy grit.

Dad fiddled with the horseshoe paperweight. "Trout and I have been talking."

Matt cleared his throat. "I've also weighed in on the conversation."

"This isn't going to turn into another situation like the wrangler fiasco, is it?" I asked.

"I don't know, kid. That depends on you," Dad replied.

Dad cut me off before I could say anything. The dimple in Matt's cheek appeared, and I raised a brow.

"Trout seems to think you've got foreman written all over you. How do you feel about that?" Dad asked.

I looked at Matt, then to Trout, and back to Dad. "I'm not sure. Matt, what do you think?"

"It's your decision. I don't think it would be much different than it is now. You're gonna continue to spout off orders to the wranglers when we're working out there anyway. And I mean that with the sincerest intent."

"So charming." I patted his hand.

Trout clicked his tongue. "You see, darlin', you've been wearing my boots for awhile. You can anticipate your daddy's thoughts, and you learned something about handling people in the last few weeks."

I turned my attention to Matt. "I'll do it under one condition."

"What's the condition?" Dad asked.

"Matt, I know you're uncomfortable taking my dad's offer right now, but would you consider learning the behind-the-scenes responsibilities when opportunities arise? If I'm gonna take on the role of foreman, I'll only do it if we're working together to make this place profitable and fabulous like Winston and Ida May groomed it to be." I shifted my gaze to my father. "Would that be okay, Dad?"

"I'd be thrilled if you two followed in my parents' footsteps," he said with a smile.

Trout raised his finger. "I second that. There ain't no shortage of brains around here. Winston and Ida May would agree."

Matt ran his fingers through his hair. "Chloe, I know how important this ranch is to you. John, I'd be honored to learn the routine without committing to the position."

Dad stood and offered his hand to Matt. "I look forward to it."

Trout stood and shook Matt's hand, too. "This old cowboy thanks you. I've got some fishing to do. By the time my cabin is finished, there'll be a path from Winston's old house to my place. You're welcome anytime." He patted Matt on the shoulder, then his gaze met mine. "Come over here, kid."

I pushed myself up from the chair and stood before him.

"I'm not riding off into the sunset just yet. The day you rode at the back of the herd with me, I knew you were ready. Any determined woman who's willing to lag behind, watch, and have a conversation without using a dictionary's dose of words can certainly fill my boots. Which I intend to wear until the day I join your grandparents, and when I do, I'm leaving those boots to you."

"That I'll have bronzed. It only seems fitting."

Trout wrapped his arms around me. He smelled like Marlboros and everything cowboy that I loved.

"Kid, the only woman I knew with a passion for riding and wrangling comparable to yours was Ida May."

"I'll remember that, cowboy." I kissed his cheek.

"Now, if you two youngsters wouldn't mind, Trout and I have some catching up to do." Dad poured to two snifters of brandy.

Trout took two cigars from his shirt pocket and handed one to Dad.

Dad sniffed it, then inspected the stamped band. "Winston's favorite."

"Things are changing around here, son." Trout patted Dad on the back like Dad did to the wranglers when he wanted them to know he appreciated their efforts or when their spirits needed lifting.

Matt and I left the room and shut the doors behind us. Matt took my hands in his.

"You did well in there, Chloe."

"Did you mean what you said about taking things slow?"

"Yep. That includes you and me."

I laced my fingers with his. "I've been thinking." The corner of my mouth lifted. "Since I'll be moving into Grandpa's house, I was wondering if you'd consider living there too?" The words came easier than I'd expected.

"You sure you want to live with a wrangler?"

I rested my forehead against his. "Yes. And you're more than just a wrangler."

"When you're ready, let me know. I'll be there." He took a hardcover book that fit neatly into the palm of his hand from his pocket. "Maggie helped me make this journal of photos for you. A little something to remind you of where you've been and where you're going."

The cover had a picture of me taking in my Montana home through the open window of Grandpa's vintage truck. I really was the spitting image of my grandmother and proud of it. I flipped through the pages taking in the scenes. The last photo was of Matt and me on our horses. Matt had written the words, *real cowboys don't let real cowgirls ride alone*, below it.

"I'm that cowboy," he said.

"It's perfect."

Matt rested his hands on my belly, and I smiled.

"You really are *that* cowboy, aren't you?"

"Yes, Chloe McIntyre, I am."

"Thank goodness, because I'm not so sure any-one else could handle me."

"You *are* a handful, but I'm up for the chal-lenge."

"That's good to know because I have some-thing to tell you." My words stuck at the back of my throat as I held his gaze.

"What's the news, Chloe?"

"We're having twins, Matt Cooper. But don't worry, cowboy, because I've got your back."

I waited for Matt to catch his breath then gave him a shiny house key that hung on a ring with a silver heart engraved with the numbers, 617. I wrapped my arms around him, and we danced, giving each other an opportunity to lead.

The Montana Bred journey continues with…

Reunion, Montana Bred, Book 2

The story of Chloe McIntyre and her mother.
Babies. Unexpected gifts and closure.

To learn more about *Reunion* …

FOLLOW ME
Linda's Website & Newsletter:
www.lindabradleyauthor.com
Linda's Amazon Author Page: amzn.to/3rzhA1G
Facebook: LBradleyAuthor
BookBub: bookbub.com/profile/linda-bradley
Instagram: lindabradleyauthor
Twitter: @LBradleyAuthor
Goodreads:
goodreads.com/author/show/6498473.Linda_Bradley

Reviews and recommendations are much
appreciated and can be submitted on Amazon,
Book Bub, or Goodreads.

NOTE TO READERS

Dear Reader,

Thank you for reading *Unbranded*. Montana holds a special place in my heart, as do readers like you!

Should you select one of my books for your book club and would like me to attend a meeting, you can email me at LBradley@LindaBradleyAuthor. com. Let me know a bit about your group, how many members you have, where you meet, and which book you've read. We can meet via cyberspace or in person, should you live local to me. If I don't respond, please reach out on social media. Glitches sometimes happen.

Feel free to send me a photo of you or your book club. I love seeing my books being read in a favorite place.

Thanks again for picking up a copy of *Unbranded*. I look forward to sharing *Reunion*, book 2 of the *Montana Bred Series* with you!

Sincerely,
Linda Bradley

Linda's Books

Maggie's Way
(Montana Bound Series Book 1)

Middle-aged Maggie Abernathy just wants to recuperate from cancer, but when Chloe and John McIntyre move in next door, somehow her empty house becomes home again.

Maggie's Fork in the Road
(Montana Bound Series Book 2)

Just when Maggie Abernathy thinks she's got her life in order, she faces loss and makes an unexpected friendship.

Maggie's Montana
(Montana Bound Series Book 3)

Maggie Abernathy makes good on a promise that changes her life forever.

A Montana Bound Christmas: Ho, Ho, Home for the Holidays!
(Montana Bound Series Book 4)

Unexpected guests and a lost dog bring the *Montana Bound Series* cast of misfits together for a special Montana Christmas.

The Montana Bound Series on Amazon: amzn.to/3rzhA1G

More by Linda

Pedal

Can a whisper from beyond give middle-aged Paula Murphy, burdened by heartache, the courage to just pedal?

Coming back to her Bay View summer home in northern Michigan means more than planning picnics at the beach and working in her daughter-in-law's bicycle shop. Her avoidance to embrace her grown son's death isn't the only tribulation weighing on this self-reliant social worker's mind.

Reluctant to believe the unfathomable, Paula Murphy's world is turned upside down when she's reunited with the only man she's ever loved.

Pedal on Amazon: amzn.to/3rzhA1G

About the Author

Linda's inspiration comes from her favorite authors and life itself. Her character-driven stories integrate humor found in everyday situations, family drama, and forever love. Her distinct voice creates memorable journeys and emotion.

Linda's been a finalist in the Booksellers Best Contest and Romance Reviews Readers' Choice Awards. She lives in Michigan with her artist husband, sons, and rescue dog. Linda loves art, animals, and stories with hope and heart.

www.ingramcontent.com/pod-product-compliance
Lightning Source LLC
Chambersburg PA
CBHW031938110726
47902CB00001B/222